✻✻✻✻✻✻✻✻✻✻✻✻✻✻✻✻✻✻✻✻✻✻✻

The SNOWS of
JASPRE

Mary Caraker

Houghton Mifflin Company
Boston   1989

The prologue of this book originally appeared in slightly altered form in *Fantasy and Science Fiction.*

Library of Congress Cataloging-in-Publication Data

Caraker, Mary.
   The snows of Jaspre / Mary Caraker.
   p.   cm.
   Summary: Morgan Farraday, an administrator from Earth, becomes
involved in the destiny of the planet Jaspre when her daughter Dee
meets the charismatic Anders Ahlwen, whose followers receive psychic
powers and transcendent spiritual reality from the artificial sun
Argus.
   ISBN 0-395-48292-5
   [1. Science fiction.]   I. Title.   88-29088
PZ7.C185Sn   1989   CIP
[fic]—dc19   AC

Printed in the United States of America

P   10 9 8 7 6 5 4 3 2 1

To Catherine, George, Richard, and Elizabeth

JASPRE

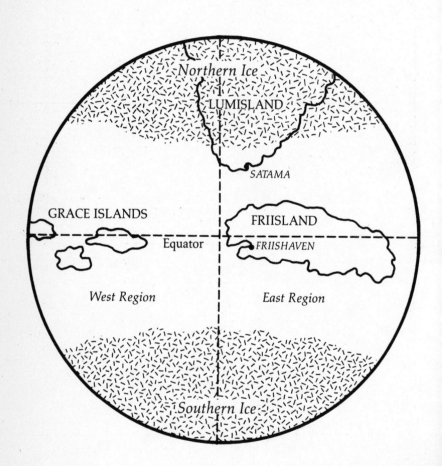

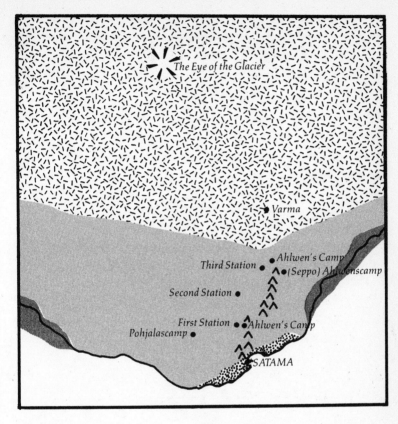

The Eye of the Glacier

Varma

Third Station · Ahlwen's Camp
∧●(Seppo) Ahlwenscamp

Second Station ·

First Station ·●Ahlwen's Camp
Pohjalascamp ·

SATAMA

⬙ Glacial Ice   ⬚ Open Tundra (Furze)

∧ Mountains   ■ Shorefast Ice

▦ Snow-covered Tundra

Southern
LUMISLAND

Prologue

Lumisland: 2301–2309

His earliest memory was of the colored snow. His mother had dressed him in warm furs and set him in front of the entrance tunnel. He reached at once for the gold and green and purple sparkles, and crowed with delight when they shimmered in his mittened hands. He tasted, and knew cold that quickly turned to pain.

His mother came at his cries and hoisted him to her hip. The other women joined in her laughter. Anders continued to scream, devastated by the betrayal.

When he was older, his mother delighted in telling the story. "Anders stuffed his mouth full of snow, like a feeding ketsi. When he started to holler, the whole camp heard him!"

Anders, even at five, didn't like to be laughed at. He knew that his father was Seppo Ahlwen, and that he was the most important man in the camp. Wasn't it called Ahlwenscamp, and wasn't it twice as large as Lahtiscamp, which he had visited once, or Jalmoscamp, where everyone lived in a single snow cave? Wasn't it his father who divided the puerhu or the hirvisen after every successful hunt? Didn't his mother wear a parka with the widest, softest ruff, and didn't she make the best fishcakes?

To young Anders, the camp was a world that couldn't possibly be improved. The half dozen houses extended like mounds from a snowbank that had formed before an up-thrusting rock formation. Part ice cave and part igloo, they faced south to obtain the warming rays of Argus. The smooth-trampled snow of the compound area in front of them was always filled with activity fascinating to a small boy. Sometimes women scraped hides and stretched them to dry on pegs. Sometimes they cut up fish or meat, slicing huge carcasses into smaller and smaller pieces without wasting a scrap. When the hunters were home, they overhauled their sleds and their skis, polishing the ice casing of the runners until they could fly over the snow with the flick of a pole. The old men worked, too, shaping antlers and tusks and bones into spear points, and the old women made snares from the fibers of puerhu flippers.

Anders and his friends played. Beyond the compound, in the unpacked snow, they built miniature houses and stalked shadowy hirvisen with imaginary spears.

The flat, snow-covered tundra stretched as far as they could see, a glowing expanse of ever-changing colors. Argus rested on the southern horizon, moving westward in a low arc, sending out the multi-hued streaks of light that transformed the snow plain.

Lumisland. It was well named, Anders thought. Lumipaikka in the old language: snowland or snowplace. Land of lights in the one they used now.

It was hard for him to believe that the snow was really white, though he had seen the true color often enough, whenever he took a handful into the house, or on the days when Argus hid behind clouds. On those dark days they stayed inside, he and his sisters. And if his father was out hunting, his mother could not eat or sleep until he arrived home safely.

His father had lost fingertips and toes to the cold. Out on the shorefast ice where he went for puerhu, winds from the northern glacier could be deadly if one's clothing failed. It was a perilous world, for all its beauty, as even the children knew.

When he was eight, Anders discovered that the world extended beyond the camps. It reached all the way to Satama, on the southern coast, where brown furze tundra showed through the snow and freefloating chunks of ice studded the shore waters.

The town nestled at the foot of a mountain that had snow only on its back slopes. It had a mud street and ugly, square houses. The patches of snow between the buildings were too dirty to reflect much color, even in the rare intervals when sleety rain did not obscure Argus.

Anders hated it from the first. His father took him to one of the flat-fronted houses with staring eyes, where he was to board for the school term. Instead of entering through a protected, upward-sloping tunnel they climbed open stairs and they had to wait in the cold in front of a door that seemed to be part of the wall.

The doors he knew were translucent curtains of puerhu gut, and the houses inside had walls and floors covered with hides and soft furs. This one was naked and much too large, and everything in it was strange. His father told him to sit on a hard-backed stool too high for his dangling legs while he talked to a man and woman.

They both looked soft and unhealthy, their faces too smooth and too pale and their clothing too thin to be of any use. His father, though, spoke to them in a tone Anders had never heard him use, as though he were not the master of Ahlwenscamp but a houseless wanderer who had to win their favor somehow.

"No, we don't want hides," the man said. "We're not a trading post. Money — you've got to pay us in money."

"I didn't know," his father said in the new, meek voice. "Where can I sell them, then?"

"Try the store," the woman said. Her mouth curved as if she was amused. *"Store:* do you know what that is?"

"Yes, I've been here before," Seppo Ahlwen said. "But I've forgotten — would you show me where?"

She pulled aside a thin covering from one of the great house eyes and pointed. "Just across the street and up." She regarded Anders curiously, with the same odd smile. "The boy can wait here. No point in his going out in that storm."

Wind-driven sleet was blowing in sheets, but Anders feared the house more. "Please, Papa," he begged. "I'll go with you."

In the store, his father was diminished again as the store-keeper sniffed at the pelts. "You're sure they're cured right? Last batch I bought went bad."

Seppo Ahlwen, whose skins were accounted the best in three camps, had to haggle like an old woman with a rancid oilcake that no one wanted. "No, I've got to pay for my boy's board," he pleaded, finally. "That won't be enough."

"Another educated grubber, eh?" The storekeeper made a sound of derision. "What's he need it for, up there in the snowdrifts? Or are you people fixin' to crawl out, finally, and live like the rest of us? About time, I'd say."

Anders's father recounted the coins and said nothing.

"Okay, then, I won't argue. Here's your price." The man added another coin to the pile. He gathered up the furs and put them behind the counter. "Maybe you'd like to take some supplies back to your camp. I've got cornmeal, potatoes, coffee. Maybe your wife'd like one of these sweaters." He held up something soft and colored like the snow. "Bring me more furs, and we can work out a trade."

His father shook his head. "I feed my family. We have what we need."

"Stubborn, eh? I heard that about you people! Anyway, I hope the boy makes out all right. It'll be tough for him. I guess you know that."

Seppo grunted, and they left the store. They stood for a moment under the shelter of the porch roof, watching the storm.

"Do I have to stay here, Papa?" Fear and despair gave Anders the daring to question a decision of his father's.

"I said it."

Anders felt a hand on his shoulder, but it was not the angry pressure he had expected. He drew more courage. "Because you went to the school once, Papa?"

5

"Partly. But I didn't stay in it long enough. You will. You won't ever be cheated by such as him." Seppo spat in the direction of the door.

They left the porch for the sleet and the slush, but the hand stayed on Anders's shoulder and the town didn't seem quite as dismal.

Anders shared a room with a boy named Peter Kantonen. Peter was twelve and came from a camp near enough that he could go home for weekends. He was kind to Anders, but the four-year difference in their ages prevented them from becoming really close. Anders was in the beginning group at school, while Peter could already read and write and do figures.

The school was one large room in its own house. Peter claimed he didn't mind it, but Anders didn't believe him. The desks where they had to sit for long hours were tortuous devices, as was the furze-fire stove that kept the room smotheringly hot. The dozen students were all from Satama except for Anders and Peter and a girl named Hulda. The three of them, Anders quickly found out, were "snowgrubbers," and fair prey for laughter and pointing fingers. One taunt, "Snowgrubber, snowgrubber, grubba dub dub," turned hurtful, concluding with his face being pushed into the schoolyard slush.

Anders's whole family, he learned, were grubbers; his whole camp. Mr. Hudson gave them a map lesson, and the world he had known shrank to nothing. There, on the wall, was all of the northern continent, Lumisland: the glacial ice cap, the snow plain, the mountains, the open tundra, and finally the harbor and the city.

Ahlwenscamp was too small to rate even a dot. Anders asked, and everyone laughed, even Peter.

For the next lesson Mr. Hudson showed them a globe that he said was their planet, Jaspre. On it, even Lumisland was insignificant. The areas where people lived were colored green, and they were all centered around Friisland, in the middle of the globe. Lumisland had a narrow green band on the southern tip, but that was all.

Anders knew the maps were wrong, but this time he kept quiet. The next lesson he dismissed as the kind of fancy old men wove into tales. It was a chart of the sky, showing suns and other planets where people lived. Mr. Hudson pointed out Terra, or Earth, which he called the Mother, and almost across the paper, Jaspre and the star that he said powered Argus. He took everyone outside on a clear day and showed them a faint white spot, low over the ocean. It was called the real sun, he said; you could see it in Friisland almost as clearly as you could see Argus. Argus was only a satellite, he said, that men had made. It collected heat and light from the real sun and beamed it down to Jaspre, which would otherwise be as cold-bitten all over as Lumisland.

He showed them pictures on a screen of Friisland and the other green places on Jaspre — fields and forests and cities that were nothing like Satama. And people — more people than Anders had ever imagined.

He didn't know where the pictures came from, but if the maps were wrong, the pictures could be, too.

7

"Milo, you used to live in Friishaven," Mr. Hudson said. "Tell the class about it."

Milo Carini's father was the manager of the fish cannery where almost everyone in Satama worked. Milo had pale skin and round eyes, and he was the leader of the boys who tormented Anders. He swaggered to the front of the room, where the screen displayed a wide, busy street and smooth-lined buildings that would dwarf even the cannery or the lodge where the ski tourists stayed.

"That's my street," Milo said. "And this house" — he pointed to the largest building, with the golden dome — "that's mine, where I lived before we came here. That's my groundcar, that I drove myself, and up there — that's my dad's flitter." He smiled smugly. "You got any questions, just ask me."

"Thank you, Milo, that will be enough," Mr. Hudson said.

Milo grinned again and strutted back down the aisle. When he passed Anders, he delivered a short, sharp kick. Mr. Hudson, as usual, didn't see it.

Anders dreamed of fighting Milo. It wasn't Milo's size that deterred him, though Milo was a head taller and thick with flesh. "You'll get sent home for good if you try it," Peter warned him. "It happened to some grubber kids before you came. That's why there's so few of us in school now."

Apparently it was all right for anyone except grubbers to fight. They had to observe every rule with scrupulous care. "They've heard things about us," Peter said. "That some of us are . . . different. They're afraid." Something in the way Mr. Hudson watched him made Anders sure that Peter was

8

right, that the teacher would prefer him not to be there.

Facing his father if he were expelled would be worse for Anders than suffering Milo. So he sat quietly, like Peter and like Hulda of the pinched face and veiled eyes, and made no trouble.

His father came for him at the end of the term. They skied northwest, over the snow plain that started on the western slope of the mountains. His father was reassuringly unchanged, with his snowburned face and shaggy furs, and so was the snow, once Argus followed them around the last peak. Surrounding them was nothing but silence and cold, shifting color: shades of violet and lichen green and the faint glitter of gold; fiery pools in every dimpled indentation; his father's track, two swaths of intense blue.

Anders pumped his legs faster to catch up. The cold hurt his throat and chest when he talked, but he tried not to show it. "I can read now, and figure." He searched his father's face for a sign of pleasure.

"So your teacher said." There was none.

At least there was no warning to back off. "Is it enough?" Anders pursued. "Do I have to go back?"

His father didn't answer for the space of so many breaths that Anders began to regret his boldness. "Of course, I didn't mind it," he lied. "Even though that teacher doesn't know so much."

His father finally turned his head. "Go on."

"He didn't even put Ahlwenscamp on his map. And he said that men made Argus, and that there are lands with no snow at all, and even crazier things. He says we always have

9

to wear something over our eyes when we're out on the snow, or we'll go blind. I'm sure he's never even seen a camp."

"Hmm." His father studied him through his slitted, heavy-lidded eyes. He slowed his pace. "Am I going too fast?"

"No." Anders himself was surprised that he was able to keep up. His breathing was no longer labored, and he was so delighted to be back again on the snow that he felt he would never tire. He waggled his skis and churned up a wake of coruscating sparkles, skied backward to watch it, and still caught up with his father.

"Enough of that," Seppo Ahlwen said. "We are going now to Pohjalascamp, and it's a long trek. You'll need all your strength."

Anders felt a prickle that was both excitement and fear. Peter had told him about the camp and about the old woman Kerttu Pohjala, who was said to be a *noita*. "Will we . . ." he started to ask, but he saw that his father's mouth was clamped tightly, a sign that the conversation was over.

They stopped twice to make hot food, pemmican in melted snow, which Seppo boiled on the folding stove from his pack. The weather was with them, remaining dry and calm. With Argus in its slow setting, undimmed by clouds, they continued to ski over the rainbow colors.

Argus was long gone from the horizon when they arrived at Pohjalascamp. In the remaining dim light, the compound was not impressive: the snow was dirty, and wrecks of sleds littered the area around a storage tent in poor repair. The dwellings consisted of a single large igloo and two smaller ones.

There was no one outside. Seppo called, and a man came out of the larger house.

"Paiva." The two men exchanged greetings in the old language. Night cold formed ice from Anders's breath, and he stamped his skis.

"No time to be out, eh, boy?" The man's grin revealed a long snaggletooth. "Come in; we're housed for the night. There's room for two more."

"Is the old woman still here?" Seppo asked. "Kerttu?"

"Ah, so that's your purpose. *Jo,* she lives over there." He pointed to the more distant of the small igloos.

"We'll see her first," Seppo said. "Then we'll be back."

Anders followed his father. "Is she a *noita*?" he asked.

"You know better than that. Or you should. There are no witches. Kerttu's always been a little crazy, from the time she lived on the glacier, but she can help folks if they'll let her. She's got healing powers, and she's got the second sight."

The prickly fear returned. "You aren't sick, are you, Papa?"

"No."

"Then why are we going to see her?"

"For you." He smiled at Anders's astonishment. "I thought you might need some healing, after all that poisonous city grub you've been eating."

His father's teasing was the only explanation Anders could get. They stopped outside the squat snowhouse, and Seppo called.

A rasping, low-pitched voice answered. "Come in, Seppo Ahlwen and Anders Ahlwen."

They removed their skis and leaned them against the wall. "How did she know who we were?" Anders whispered.

"I told you." Seppo stepped over the sill and crouched as he passed through the short tunnel. He parted the puerhu curtain and disappeared inside.

Anders followed close behind. In the room, a glowing oilring stove cast dancing shadows over the face of the old woman who sat cross-legged on a bed of furs. It was a face snowburned almost black, seamed and pitted and with all the signs of age: the sunken mouth, the eyes hidden behind drooping folds of flesh.

She motioned for them to sit. "So, Seppo, you have come back. You still do not believe?" She had a man's voice, rough and gravelly, as if it had been injured.

"I thought you should see the boy again. The other time, he was only a baby."

"Come here, then." She beckoned to Anders.

He squatted in front of her. She reached out with bony hands and described an arc in the air around him. "Look at me."

Her eyes were pinpoints of light, and as he stared into them he saw a reflection of all the colors of Argus. He saw, too, not in her eyes but in his own mind, an ice plateau, brilliant under Argus's light.

"There is a place on the glacier," she whispered, "where all the colors come together. All the powers of Argus, in one spot, waiting to be taken in."

She moved her hands, making the arc larger, and it seemed to Anders that something inside him swelled, too, and thrummed for release.

She lowered her hands and turned to Seppo. "Nothing is changed."

"I've sent him to school," Seppo said. "I thought per-haps —"

"It will fill his head and drive out the other?" Her laugh-ter was a harsh explosive sound, like the bark of a ketsi.

It ended in a racking cough. She waved her hands, brush-ing at the air. "Go away, both of you," she croaked between paroxysms. "The school is useless. It would be better for him to go at once to the ice." She turned from them to cough again, gut-wrenching spasms that shook her narrow frame.

She continued to show them her back, rocking herself and mumbling words that Anders could not understand.

They left, to Anders's great relief. "She's very ill," Seppo said outside.

"Why can't she make herself well, if she's a healer?" An-ders asked. He had many other questions, but he was afraid to voice them.

"Perhaps she's too old" is all that Seppo would say.

That night, in the big igloo, Anders could not sleep. He listened to the snores around him, wondering about Kerttu and the odd way she had made him feel.

Her words, too, remained with him. Saying he should go to the ice. No one went out on the glacier unless they were slightly mad, like Kerttu. Then, they seldom returned.

He knew of the glacier. It had no tundra under it, no lichen for animals to feed on. It had winds that would knock a man off his feet, and crevasses that would swallow him. The colors of Argus were said to be incomparable there, but not even his father, who was the bravest man he knew, would venture there to see them.

13

He had heard talk of a man from Jalmoscamp who had come back from the glacier so crazed that on a puerhu hunt he had walked over new ice into the ocean. He had heard other stories, whispered at night around fires, about men who had become cannibal creatures.

It was impossible to think that he would ever go there. He agreed with Kerttu that the school was useless, but the other — it made no sense at all.

His father said nothing more about the visit to Kerttu, not during the entire remainder of the long trek home, but Anders could tell that he too was troubled. He could feel his father watching him, measuring him, even when they both had their eyes fixed on the shifting colors ahead.

Seppo set a hard pace, for Pohjalascamp had been out of their way, and they still had almost three days' skiing ahead of them. Anders strained at first to keep up. He would show his father, he determined, panting and pushing.

After a time, however, it became less and less of an effort. Strength flowed into him as the colors of Argus flowed together before his eyes, and he skimmed the snow as easily as if he were in flight before the wind.

Once he even shot into the lead.

It was this time he felt his father's gaze most strongly, and there was no approval in it. Anders fell back to his old position, wondering at the grim line of his father's mouth. He hadn't expected praise — it wasn't Ahlwen's way — but Anders thought that he might have said something, perhaps to the effect that now Anders was so strong and fast, it was time for him to go on his first hunt. Boys not much older than he had gone. Anders could pull a sled with the men;

he knew he could. He could throw a spear and he could keep up with anyone.

But his father said nothing. They sheltered late that night in the snow patrol shed at Second Station. The lodge was full of tourists, and Anders and Seppo rose early to avoid the power sleds that screamed and churned gouges in the smooth surface of the snow. Seppo did not light the stove for breakfast; they had a swallow of water from the buried flask and chewed on strips of jerky that they had kept soft under their clothing. They made Third Station by the second night, and in the morning turned east. The mountains were low here, with an easy pass. Anders had no trouble with the climb, and coming down in the late afternoon he could see the camp ahead: the rocks and the snow bank with its protruding mounds, the domes more glittering than the one in the school picture. He saw his little sisters playing at the edge of the compound, pulling a toy sled fashioned from a curved piece of bone.

"Bekka! Karin!" he called. "You have a new doll! But that sled — never mind about it, Bekka, don't cry. I'll make you a better one when I get there."

"Anders!" His father shouted and poked him with a ski pole. "Stop that! You can't hear them. You can't even see them from here." His jaw was hard again, his face dark.

Anders blinked, and it was true. The camp was still a distant smudge, barely discernible in the wash of late-day colors. "I . . . thought I saw —"

"You imagined it," his father said. He was calmer now. "The light can play tricks like that, especially when you've been out all day."

Anders had seen mirages before, but this had been different. He did not refute his father, however.

When they skied into the camp, he saw that it had been no trick. The sled was broken, and Bekka's doll was exactly as he had seen it: a carved ivory head and a dress made from the downy fur of a baby ergip.

His mother hugged him and laughed and cried. She had saved dinner: his favorite fish stew flavored with sinop, and mealcakes from one of her precious sacks. His sisters stared at first, but soon they were climbing all over him as they had always done. It was very late when they spread their furs for sleep.

His mother's voice woke him. "That *noita*! I don't believe a word of what she said. I never have."

"Shhh!" There was stillness again, then his father's whisper. "You can see how he's changed already. He can outski me, and who knows what goes on in his head. No, he has to leave the snow, it's the only way. It was a mistake bringing him home this time, and I won't make it again."

The whispers continued, but Anders pressed his hands to his ears so he couldn't hear any more.

He rolled himself into a tight ball as his world crumbled. His father didn't want him! That was why he had been sent away, and the next time it would be for good.

It was unthinkable, unbearable. But it was the truth.

Subsequent days did not prove Anders wrong. His father seldom spoke to him — seldom, in fact, appeared even to see him. The men prepared for the hirvisen hunt, and his uncles and the other fathers schooled their sons in wind patterns, in throwing spears, and in vital target points. Anders hung around and listened, but no one invited him to participate. When they left, the boys hiding their pride and the men their excitement, Anders was alone, the only one of his cousins and former playmates who remained with the women and the old men and little children.

He thought he would never get over the shame. His mother cooked treats for him every day, even though their stores were low, and called him the "camp protector," but he knew better. Camp outcast was more like it. The hunters returned with three large animals, and he stayed inside during the butchering. Everyone would have a story, he knew; even the lookouts and the shouters who turned the herd. Especially his cousin Karl, who was six months younger than he, and a braggart.

His father came into the igloo. "Help your mother," he said. So Anders had to listen, after all, while he scraped hides with the women.

He stayed behind, too, when the men went to the ocean ice for fish and puerhu. This time Karl and the younger boys did not go, but Anders no longer ranged with them over the snow. When he wasn't alone he spent his time with Bekka and Karin, who delighted in his attention and knew nothing about his change of status.

The men returned, and Seppo announced that it was time for Anders to leave again for Satama. He would not have believed it possible a scant three months ago, but Anders felt as much relief as sadness. His mother clutched him and stroked his face as if she never expected to see him again, and that was a bad moment. But then his father shouted, and there was no kindness in his voice. Anders followed him from the camp without once looking backward.

This time his father accompanied him only as far as Third Station, where Anders was to go on by jetsled to Satama. Seppo's goodbyes were short and businesslike; he told his son where money would be sent and that letters he wished to write should be addressed to Third Station. "I understand, if you do well in the Satama school, there is SEF money, government money, to send you to Friishaven. You must try for it."

Nothing about ever coming home. His father even took his skis, as if to cut off that possibility of return. He hates me, Anders told himself, and he tried not to think about it to keep from disgracing himself with tears.

Anders was alone with the driver until Second Station, when the sled filled with returning snow tourists. He huddled in the end of a rear seat, too miserable to appreciate the new sensation of effortless travel. The fare, he knew, had cost Seppo six ketsi pelts. It must have been important to him, Anders thought. Terribly important, to avoid spending three days in his son's company.

He was in Satama by late afternoon, back in his old room. Peter was not there. He was living at the lodge, his landlady said. He had a job there, and he would not be back in school.

Anders tramped up the hill to see Peter. Satama was just as ugly as before, the streets as muddy and the sky as gray. The road to Lumisatama Lodge wound up the mountain behind the town, a steep climb even with switchbacks. Rain sheeted in from the ocean before Anders was halfway, and his furs were dripping when he reached the entrance to the lodge.

He was directed to the kitchen, where his former roommate was scrubbing pots from the evening meal. It seemed to Anders that Peter had grown six inches. He was the height of a man, but he still had smooth cheeks that flushed when he saw Anders. "This is just a part of my job," he said at once. "The worst part. As soon as I finish here, I get to do the best, helping the guide when the guests go out for the late-color skiing." He scrubbed at a last blackened pan, rinsed and dried it, and took off his apron. "Maybe you can come along, if there's room in the sled. The first-timers always need a hand with their skis."

"Well . . . sure." All last year in school, Anders hadn't been out on the snow. That was one reason the year had been so bad.

"You wait here. I'll ask." Peter hurried off, and Anders waited nervously by the door.

A man looked in from the adjoining room and beckoned. He had a grubber face, but was wearing Satama snowgear. "You the boy? Come on, then, we're ready to go."

Anders followed him to the porch. Peter was waiting, wearing a new city parka. "Pick a pair that fits you," the man said to Anders, indicating the rack of skis. The sled was already loaded, and he and Peter and Anders grabbed the handholds and perched precariously outside.

The sled took them through town on slow pulse power, then around the mountain to the slopes and the beginning of the snow plain. It was dry here, and Argus hung shimmering in its final burst of color. The sun-construct was surrounded by three halos: a first full one of deep purple, then a three-quarter one of carmine, and a final half circle of molten gold. On the slopes, concentric patterns of like colors spread into the dusk of the north, while underfoot the snow crystals gleamed like miniature jewels.

The tourists gasped and ahed. They all wore face masks, though there was no wind, and dark wraparound goggles that made Anders wonder how much they could actually see. Anders and Peter helped them secure their skis and rode herd on the line once the guide led them off.

The line moved slowly at first, and Anders ranged up and down, offering encouragement where it was needed.

Peter skied up to him, masked and goggled like one of the tourists. "Not a bad job, eh?"

"Why are you wearing those?" Anders asked.

Peter adjusted the woolen mask. "You should, too, unless you want to look like a grubber forever."

"Nothing can change that."

"Sure you can. There's no need to be snowburned. And it makes them" — he nodded toward the line of skiers — "less nervous about you. They've heard funny things about grubber eyes."

Anders wasn't sure if he liked this new Peter. "So what happens when you go back to your camp?"

"I'm never going back. Not to live, anyway. Why should I, as long as I can earn my keep here?" Peter dug in his poles and scooted off.

Another outcast, Anders thought. But Peter was apparently a willing one. In school, he had always tried to be like the town kids.

Not me, Anders vowed. He had decided it as soon as he was back in the mud of Satama. He would live on the snow again someday, even if he had to start his own camp.

The colors, as always, glowed most brightly just before Argus sank. When Anders looked through Peter's goggles, the hues were dimmed by half. He gave the glasses back hurriedly, unwilling to miss a fraction of the spectacle. As he herded the tourists back to the sled he felt the colors warm within him, almost as if he were back in Ahlwens-camp in the days when his father had loved him.

Several of the tourists gave him coins, and the guide said he could come again. Knowing he was welcome somewhere made the night bearable, back in the hard-walled room.

In school, he was in a more advanced group than before, but the lessons were much easier. To escape notice, he pretended to labor over them like everyone else. He could have given perfect answers to every recitation. He knew what Mr. Hudson's questions would be before the teacher even asked them, but again he dissembled.

He never raised his hand. In fact, he seldom spoke at all. Milo Carini still led the grubber-baiting gang, and Anders was careful to do nothing to provoke them. The one time he had reached out to protect himself, he had sent a town boy flying halfway across the slushy yard.

It had frightened Anders more than the boy, who was fortunately unhurt. It could have been much worse, Anders knew.

You can see how he's changed already. Anders thought often

21

about his father's words. He returned from the skiing each night with his head buzzing, and every day in school it became harder to hold back his growing abilities.

Three months into the term, a visitor came to the school. He wore shiny boots and a green uniform, the same kind Anders had seen in the films Mr. Hudson had been showing with his new machine.

"We have a visitor today from SEF," Mr. Hudson said. He printed the letters on the chalkboard. "Engineering Corpsman Keefer, from Space Exploratory Forces." The teacher's eyes warned: best behavior, all of you, if you know what's good for you.

Anders sat up straight, like everyone else in the room. SEF, that gave orders to even the Jasprian High Council!

The corpsman smiled. "This isn't an official inspection. Nothing like that. You can relax, all of you."

No one moved, and Mr. Hudson continued to twist his fingers nervously.

Corpsman Keefer took off his helmet and unbuttoned the stiff collar of his jacket. He had curly red hair and a pink-toned, friendly face. "I was sent here to ask questions of some of the students, but it has nothing at all to do with schoolwork. No one is being tested."

Mr. Hudson cleared his throat. "I'm sure everyone will cooperate."

The corpsman searched the room with his eyes. "Actually, I only want to talk to those children who come from the snow country. Whose families live there." He studied each face. "You . . . and you." He indicated Hulda and Anders. "You're both snowgrubbers, aren't you?"

Hulda looked down, as she always did, and Anders too studied the top of his desk.

"Answer him!" Mr. Hudson said sharply. Eliciting no response, he turned to the visitor. "Yes, they're grubbers. The only two I have this term."

"Is there someplace I could speak to them privately?"

The teacher shrugged. "There's just the one room, as you see." Outside it was sleeting.

"Then, could I use your desk and a couple of chairs?" Keefer quickly arranged a semiprivate corner. He beckoned to Hulda and Anders.

"What do you know of the history of Jaspre?" he asked when they were settled.

Neither answered.

"Did you know that your people — the so-called grubbers — were the original settlers?"

Anders finally looked up. "The ones who spoke the old language?"

"Yes. Finnish, it was called. One of the pre-space Earth languages. Your ancestors were here even before Argus went up. Jaspre was considered then to be a hardship colony, and there weren't many takers. But those hardy Finn grubbers stuck it out, and even seemed to like it. When SEF put up Argus and terraformed Friisland, they retreated to Lumisland so they could live the way they were used to. With a present from Argus, of course, that no one had expected — the colored snow.

23

"Now we're wondering if Argus might have given us another gift as well. We've heard of 'special' people among the grubbers. People with unusual powers. Do either of you know of any?"

Hulda stared impassively at a spot on the floor. She shook her head.

"And you?" He looked at Anders. "Have you heard of anyone who can see farther than most people? Maybe even see into the future? Someone who can tell what others are thinking? Who can heal a wound or move something without lifting a finger? Perhaps only someone who is unusually strong?"

The friendly pink face smiled encouragingly, but behind the smile Anders saw a scene that chilled him: a stark, white-walled room filled with shining tables and machines with clicking eyes and wiry tentacles.

It was warning enough. "No," he said. "No one. Not ever."

The SEF corpsman sighed. "Do you suppose I could arrange to visit a camp?"

Anders did not answer, nor did Hulda.

Flushing, the corpsman arose. "That's all," he said, dismissing the two.

"Are they always that uncommunicative?" Anders heard him ask Mr. Hudson.

"Grubbers!" the teacher said.

Anders stared at the black case of his reader, too shaken to even pretend to study. He knew now what he was, and what his father had tried to prevent, and the knowledge washed away a shored-up wall of bitterness.

He was trying to save me, Anders thought. Not from the

Friishaven laboratory — his father knew nothing of that — but from the danger he did know: Kerttu's way, the way of the glacier.

Lovingly meant, but futile. Anders knew now he could no more escape the snow than he could stop breathing. Nor would he want to. He glanced up at the globe of Jaspre on Mr. Hudson's desk, at the tiny area that was the polar continent of Lumisland. With his other vision he saw Lumisland glow until it lit up the entire sphere. Whatever awaited him on the glacier, in that nexus where all the colors came together, he would be ready for it and he would welcome it.

He spent the rest of the afternoon designing grubber camps where icehouses gleamed and where lichen and sinop roots flourished under the snow in sheltered, Argus-lit glades. He also indulged himself in a long-deferred satisfaction — a faster-than-sight spitwad aimed dead center at the back of Milo Carini's head.

✳1✳

Friisland: 2390

The air had a bite to it, something sharp and faintly metallic that stung Morgan's nose when she awoke in the mornings. She had been assured that she would get used to it, and indeed the permanent residents of Jaspre claimed it was not noticeable. But after a week Morgan still woke to sneezes and a headache. The discomfort went away, though, within an hour, and she counted herself lucky — her husband, Arnie, suffered until noon. Her son, Matt, felt nothing at all.

The boy was dressed and at the front window when Morgan, still in her robe, came into the living room. She stood beside him to catch the spectacle of Argus as it burst over the city horizon in a prism of light. The distant real sun had already risen in the opposite sky, visible from the back rooms, but it was too ordinary a sight to interest either Morgan or Matt. Argus, however, had not yet ceased to fascinate them.

Morgan tightened her arm around Matt's shoulders as the

sun-construct colored the sky with a display of multi-hued, brilliant streaks. As she watched, she marveled anew at the triumph of SEF engineering. Risen, Argus became to all appearances a small, bright sun, but Morgan tried to imagine it as it really was: a giant wheel studded with a hundred radiant eyes; a heat-beaming satellite that revolved around glacial Jaspre to warm its equatorial zones to a temperate climate.

Matt turned from the window, and Morgan dropped her arm. Matt was ten, and already beginning to be embarrassed by displays of maternal affection.

"What will happen to us here if Argus ever goes out?" he asked.

"It's not likely," Morgan replied. "Argus is powered by the real sun. You know: they explained it to us at the monitoring station."

"I just wondered, 'What if?' What it would be like."

Morgan sneezed and reached for a tissue. "You'll find out when we visit the snow zones. That's how it used to be all over Jaspre, and people did live here. Not comfortably, like we do now, and not very many of them. I understand there are still some hardy souls pioneering it out there."

"Will we see them?"

"Maybe, though we'll be staying in one of the lodges and not out in the wilderness." She couldn't resist a pat to the stubborn cowlick that stood up on Matt's forehead. "It's always been a dream of mine, to see the snow under Argus light. If there really are colors in it."

"Mine, too," Matt agreed as he ducked from under her

hand. He scowled at the empty room. "When are we going to get the rest of our furniture? And where's Dad? Isn't he up yet?"

Morgan started for the kitchen. "I'm going to call supply about the sofa and chairs as soon as I get to the office. They were promised yesterday. And Arnie's already gone. He had to get to the spaceport early."

A wide smile spread across Matt's face. "He got a job there?"

"No, but he heard that they might be hiring in security, and he wanted to be the first to apply."

"Oh, he'll get on, then," the boy said with easy confidence. "Maybe they'll even put him in charge, like he was on Hedron II." He took down plates and started to set the table.

Morgan stopped him. "Just juice and food cubes this morning, I'm afraid. I have to get ready for work, and I haven't time to cook."

"Dad fixes a *real* breakfast."

"Ha! If he gets this job, young man, your pampered days will be over."

Matt wasn't the only one who had been pampered lately, she thought. It was great for her, having a househusband, but in all fairness she hoped it would end soon. Arnie hadn't anticipated how difficult it would be to find work in Friishaven, and repeated failures were beginning to take their toll on his humor. On New Terra he had been a colony leader, and before that, with SEF, he had held responsible positions. Morgan guessed how he must feel now, encountering nothing but rejection.

She made a silent wish that today his luck would change. She downed her own juice, checked her watch, and excused herself; she had fifteen minutes to shower and dress.

She was running late, and chose her green Corps uniform because it was quicker than assembling another outfit. Besides, she was new to her position, and her show of service emblems established her as a seasoned professional. Morgan was well into middle age, but thanks to good health and lucky genes, she looked considerably younger. Sometimes it was a problem.

Though she had taught in Space Corps schools on a variety of worlds, this was only Morgan's second stint as an administrator and the first in which she was responsible for the schools in an entire region. She knew that if she failed she would be out to pasture for good. It hadn't been easy, convincing the Corps to give her another assignment at an age when she should have been contentedly retired, and she was determined to prove that they hadn't made a mistake. Of course, she and Arnie had the farm on New Terra to fall back on, but neither of them was ready yet to be planetbound. With Dee and Danny at the SEF Academy on Earth, and Matt eager for adventure, this posting had seemed ideal for all of them.

No, Morgan vowed, she would make it work. She twisted her brown hair into a businesslike bun, loaded her carrycase with the files she had reviewed last night, and placed a call for bus pickup.

"Arnie took the flitter," she said to Matt. "I have to leave now, going by ground. You'll get to school on time, won't you?"

"Sure. I've got an hour. I can even walk."

"You know the way?"

"Mom! I've only been there a dozen times already!"

She smiled at his exasperation. "Okay. You lock up then, and I'll see you later." She mouthed a kiss and opened the door.

"Mom."

She turned back.

"Why are you wearing your hair so funny?"

On the bus, she loosened the bun. Kids! she thought. But maybe he was right; she should relax and be herself, and not worry about images.

The bus rolled smoothly through the wide streets of Friishaven. The capital of East Region was a port city of uniform, low buildings interspersed with park blocks and water blocks and straight, sparkling canals. The traffic on both ground and air was sparse and orderly. The few pedestrians were well dressed and all were Earth-standard human.

A well-planned city, Morgan granted, though it might have been designed with more imagination. As was true of the terraformed countryside that spread beyond the harbor. She pictured the unnaturally symmetrical landscape of the island continent of Friisland as she had viewed it from the shuttle: forests marching in neat rows of trees, reservoir-lakes glistening in perfect squares and ovals, rivers running ribbon-straight through manicured grasslands, and even the mountains looking somehow sculpted.

It was all a bit disappointing to Morgan — not the exotic Jaspre she had expected. But that strange frozen world, she knew, lay just beyond the warming range of Argus. There would be time enough to see it when she had established herself firmly in her post.

Morgan's tiny office in the SEF building looked out upon an unpainted wall, reminding her that though she might be high in the ranks of the teaching corps, in the wheels of its parent Space Exploratory Forces she was a very minor cog.

Her secretary, whom she shared with the adjoining records office, was busy over there. As Morgan unpacked her case, the faces of her nineteen-year-old twins stared at her from the holos on her desk: Danny sternly and Dee with her shy, sweet smile. In the one letter that had arrived from Earth, Dee had sounded unhappy. The Academy was tough, Morgan knew from experience. She wondered if it had been the right choice for Dee.

Useless to worry now, she told herself. Beginnings were always hard; Dee would adjust.

Morgan had her own beginnings to deal with. She called up more files from her computer and printed them out. The first task she had set herself was to become familiar with every school and teacher in her region, and she had made a fair start on paper. Next, she would plan visits. She worked through lunch, eating from a tray at her desk. In the afternoon she was scheduled for a conference of SEF headquarters personnel.

This was the first time Morgan had seen all two dozen of the SEF staff assembled. Commander Nurmi presided, though his aide, Lieutenant DiVoto, made the actual presentation. The commander's unblinking eyes dominated a heavy-jowled, bulldog face. He was a man of few words, as Morgan had discovered at her first interview. DiVoto, on the other hand, was a charmer: young (late twenties, Morgan guessed), almost as handsome as a Tri-V idol, with a relaxed manner and a grin that couldn't be resisted.

DiVoto was all business, however, as he introduced the topic, "A Second Argus: Pros and Cons." Everyone else seemed to be familiar with the proposal, and Morgan listened attentively as the lieutenant presented a number of reports on the feasibility of putting up another sun-construct.

The proposed new, smaller satellite would be orbited above the northern snow zone, greatly expanding the habitable portions of Lumisland. Though she could understand little of the technical language, Morgan easily grasped the main problem: whether any increase in the size of the habitable zones would justify the enormous problems of managing the glacial run-off.

The Argus engineers were strongly in favor of the project, pointing to the successful operation of Argus One. The reports of the terraforming specialists were less positive. In their studies of how the glacial melt of Argus Two would affect the existing land masses, they stressed the dangers of unmanageable floods. The ice cap that covered the northern quarter of the planet would be reduced by half, they predicted, and Lumisland would lose a portion of its southern coast to an ice-free ocean. In exchange, however, the great northern continent would gain a hundred thousand square miles of potentially arable land.

In the area warmed by Argus One, the temperature of Friisland and the Grace Islands would be raised ten to fifteen degrees. There could be no assurance of safety for the coastal settlements. In fact, the most cautious of the experts advocated a temporary evacuation of the entire planet, and Morgan thought with dismay about packing up again. She hoped it wouldn't be soon.

When DiVoto opened the matter to discussion, Morgan said nothing. The majority seemed to favor the project. The more colonists, the more administrative jobs for SEF. But there was some concern over the reactions of the Friisland settlers, who had heard rumors of the project and were reportedly uneasy. "I'd like to know who leaked this," the commander growled. "It was classified and shouldn't have gotten out of the building."

There were no comments. "Of course, the final decision will come from Earth," the lieutenant said in closing. "We'll forward all these reports, along with Commander Nurmi's recommendations. He thanks you for your input."

The commander compressed his lips. Morgan had the feeling that he had made up *his* mind about Argus Two long before the meeting, and that some of what he had heard hadn't pleased him. He left hurriedly.

DiVoto remained to gather up his slides and papers. The other participants filed out, a few with troubled expressions that matched Morgan's.

"You look worried, Farraday." The lieutenant closed his case and beckoned to Morgan.

"Does it show? I'm afraid I'm taking a short view, hoping I won't have to leave before I've even properly seen the planet."

He gave a hint of a smile. "No danger of that. Even if Argus Two is approved, the construction itself would take years. As for the lobbying and the fund-raising — you know how that can drag on. No, you're safe enough here for all the sightseeing you care to do."

Morgan felt her face flame. How stupid of her! Of course she knew better, but she had spoken without thinking. A bubble-headed tourist, that's how she must appear to him!

She could see no way to extricate herself. "Yes, of course," she said stiffly, and started for the door.

"Wait, I . . ." DiVoto bit his lip. "I didn't mean to . . ." He appeared as embarrassed as she.

His own distress freed her. "It's okay," she said with a laugh. "I'm really not as dumb as I sound, though sometimes I wonder. It's just a case of foot-in-mouth disease. I suffer from it a lot."

"We all do, sometimes," he said. "But I wouldn't worry about your case. It couldn't be serious, not when you're a regional supervisor at your age. I'm impressed."

She should have kept the bun, Morgan thought. But no — why not enjoy the admiration in his eyes? "You appear to be successful yourself, Lieutenant DiVoto," she said. "You handled that meeting awfully well."

"Thanks. And the name is Justin." His eyes crinkled. "Welcome to our stalwart band. If I can help you in any way . . ."

Morgan smiled her appreciation. "I may take you up on it. There's so much I don't know." They parted at adjoining corridors, and Morgan returned to her office.

Jazmin Rey, Morgan's secretary, looked up from her desk. "How was the meeting? The usual fascinating batch of statistics about the grain harvest?"

"No, it was all about Argus Two. Justin DiVoto —"

"Ah. First names already." Jazmin quirked a carefully painted black eyebrow. She was a tall, dark-haired woman with olive skin, strong, striking features, and a tendency to the florid in her dress and makeup. Today she wore black skinthins with a red flower in her high-coiled hair.

Morgan both liked her and appreciated the efficient way she ran two offices, not to mention her unending font of information on everyone in the building. "Okay, spill," she said. "Does the lieutenant have a dangerous reputation? I can imagine, with his looks . . ."

Jazmin tapped her pencil on an inch-long, silver fingernail. "Oddly enough, no," she said. "He's not married, and he's been the target of more campaigns than I can count. It's sort of a female rite of passage here, falling for Justin. But as far as I know, he's kept his office life as clean as a whistle. In town, now, who knows? There's no scandalous gossip, though." She regarded Morgan quizzically. "So it's your turn?"

"Absolutely not!" Morgan flushed. "Arnie and I — we're solid."

"Good. I like Arnie."

"Which reminds me . . ." Morgan reached for the phone. Arnie might be home, and she was anxious to hear about the job interview.

She knew the bad news as soon as she saw his face on the visiplate. "They'll put me on the list, and call. But we both know what that means. It's the same story, honey: they won't take on someone my age."

Morgan tried to cheer him, but there was little she could

say. She hung up feeling depressed herself. And blame-worthy. If Arnie had known how long the job search would be for him, he might not have been so willing to leave New Terra. He had always been more content there than she, attending council meetings and planting his crops, and she had to admit that the responsibility for their move was primarily hers.

At least he shouldn't have to rattle around in an empty house; the visiplate had revealed that there was still no furniture in the living room. She called supply and badgered them until they promised to deliver it immediately.

Her guilt somewhat lightened, she returned to work. Jazmin was hers for the afternoon, so she dictated letters and let the secretary guide her through the maze of bureaucratic forms required to inaugurate her school visiting program. Jazmin left at four-thirty sharp, but Morgan stayed to meet with a parents group. By the time she heard the last of their grievances, it was long past normal working hours, and when she left the office both Argus and the sun were sinking.

Thank God Arnie was home, she thought as she rode a ground bus that seemed interminably slow. At least Matt wasn't alone. He had said he wouldn't mind the Youth Center after school, but Morgan knew he preferred to be with his father.

Through the window on her side, Morgan watched Argus stain the sky in a final burst of color as it disappeared. The satellite made two revolutions of Jaspre for every rotation of the planet, so the day-night periods were Earth-normal. Morgan tried to imagine the proposed second Argus, traveling low in the opposite direction, and counted the number of times it would rise and set. There would be dim Argus light for two periods during the night, and the days would be considerably warmer. Friisland would be almost tropical, and in the north there would be vast new lands.

Yet there was the cost, and the danger, and the disruption of people's lives.

NO ARGUS TWO. She saw the sign posted in a lighted store window, and now that she understood its meaning she remembered seeing similar notices around town. What position would she take, she wondered, if she were a permanent resident here? She had never been one to choose the safe and the known, at least not until she had acquired a family. Now, she too might prefer the status quo.

The bus turned onto her street, which was lined with one-family woodplas bungalows and patches of yard. The house was lighted but quiet. Inside, the new furniture was in place, arranged stiffly along the walls. Morgan pushed two chairs into a cozier grouping and pictured a colored throw on the sofa. She called out for Arnie.

"Shhh!" He came from the back hall with his finger to his lips. Matt, round-eyed, followed at his heels.

"We have a visitor," Arnie said as he closed the sliding door behind him. "A very tired one, and she's just gone to bed."

"It's Dee," Matt explained before Arnie could. "She came in on the shuttle and she's left the Academy and she cried when Dad asked her why. Now she's making funny noises in her sleep."

2

Arnie refused to discuss Dee in Matt's presence, so Morgan had to wait until the boy went reluctantly to bed. Dee was sleeping on a cot in the room they had intended for a study, and when Morgan looked in on her she was shocked by the thin white face and the bruiselike purple shadows beneath her eyes. She had been round-cheeked and rosy when Morgan had seen her off to Earth less than two months ago, and Morgan could hardly believe the change.

"What happened? Why is she here?" she asked as soon as she and Arnie were alone.

Arnie built a furze-block fire in the stove, frowning as he adjusted the vents. When he turned to Morgan, his face was deeply furrowed. "She didn't tell me much, except that she hated Earth and that she'd been sick. She withdrew everything from her Academy account and borrowed from Danny to get here by hypership."

"Sick? How?"

"Headaches. It seems they started on the trip out. A reaction to hyperspace, the doctors at the Academy told her. The headaches should have gone away, but they didn't. She couldn't keep up with her studies, panicked, and here she is."

A sound from the study alerted both of them. "I'll go," Morgan said.

Dee was still asleep, but moaning and twitching and clutching at her coverlet. Morgan stroked her forehead and whispered soothing words until she quieted. Could it be her old injury? Morgan wondered. As a child, Dee had fallen from a pedway overpass, but they had all been assured that the latest techniques of regenerative surgery had repaired the damage to her brain tissues. And she had shown no ill effects up to now.

She had been such a loving child, eager to please. Perhaps, Morgan thought, Dee had merely been trying to imitate her when she chose the Academy. Danny had never wavered in his ambitions for a SEF career, but Morgan suspected now that Dee had simply done what was expected of her.

Arnie had been so proud. I was too, Morgan admitted to herself. She smoothed a skein of fine, blond hair that lay tangled on the pillow. "I should have drawn you out more," she whispered. "I should have found out what you really wanted."

Arnie appeared in the doorway, and Morgan left the bedside. "She seems to be in pain or distress," she said when they were settled again in front of the fire. "You say she had a complete physical on Earth?"

"Yes, including a brain scan."

"And they didn't find anything?"

"According to Dee, no. But I'm taking her to the hospital here tomorrow, to find out for myself."

Arnie refused to meet her eyes, but his tight mouth told Morgan that he shared her own worst fears.

"Don't," she said. She reached for his hands, and he answered her pressure.

They took what comfort they could from each other. In bed, Morgan lay awake for hours, listening for Dee and wondering just how ill she really was.

In the morning, Morgan heard Dee singing in the shower. It couldn't be too bad, she thought. Dee came into the kitchen and ran into Morgan's arms.

"Dee!" "Mom!" they exclaimed together.

In the past year, Dee had taken to calling her mother by her first name, and the more intimate term warmed Morgan. However, she didn't like Dee's shadowed eyes, and she couldn't help commenting on her thinness. "I know dorm food isn't the greatest. All those starches, I remember. But still, most of us gained on it."

Dee took a place at the table. "I couldn't eat it at all," she said. She gasped over the plate of golden eggs that Arnie set in front of her. "Now this is more like it!" She tasted a mouthful, then pushed the remainder around with her fork.

"Hyperspace," Arnie said. "It takes a while to get back your appetite."

"Can I have them?" Matt asked. He had polished off his own portion in less than a minute.

"I see your manners haven't improved, suction mouth," Dee said, laughing. She passed him her plate.

"So you didn't like it at all on Earth?" Morgan asked.

"I hadn't realized how crowded it would be. There was never a chance to be alone."

"What about Danny?" Arnie asked.

"He didn't mind it so much. But then, he was always studying, and I don't think he even noticed anything around him. Certainly not me."

Morgan and Arnie both looked up at the note of bitterness, and Dee made a shamefaced moue. "Forget I said that. I was a drag for Danny. Mooning around homesick. Doped up with pills for my headaches, in the infirmary half the time. I think he was relieved when I decided to leave." She looked around the table at each one of them, and her slow smile lit her face. "You don't know how good it is to be here. It's so . . . peaceful. Almost like New Terra. Like home. I slept better last night than I have in months, and you know, my head isn't even hurting anymore."

"You won't mind, though, having another checkup here?" Though he put it as a question, it was clear that Arnie expected agreement.

Some of Dee's brightness faded. "Sure. Whatever you say." Her eyes shifted apprehensively from Arnie to Morgan. "If they don't find anything . . . I know the doctors at the Academy thought I was just pretending."

"We wouldn't think that," Morgan assured her. "I could tell last night that you were in pain."

"Are you disappointed in me, for not sticking it out?" The anxiety was still there.

"Dee, I love you, and I'm glad you're here. No more nonsense, now, about 'disappointed.' " When Arnie didn't

41

second her immediately, Morgan nudged him under the table.

"Of course. Your health is all that's important." Arnie reached to pat Dee's hand, and she responded by bursting into tears.

Morgan led her into Matt's room and held her until the sobbing stopped. Dee mopped her face and sat on the bed. "I'm so ashamed," she said.

Morgan sat beside her. She's pregnant, she thought. Then: No, not sober, responsible Dee. "Ashamed of what?" she asked gently. When Dee didn't respond, she prodded. "Whatever it is, it can't be so terrible that we wouldn't understand. You can tell me. Really."

Dee tore at her wadded, wet tissue. "But it isn't anything I can put into words. I feel awful that I've let everyone down. I was always such a good student before. Everyone said — you said — that I should set my sights as high as I could. I tried to do it, but at the Academy I just couldn't seem to function. There were the headaches, of course, but it was more than that. It was as if I wasn't myself at all." Her voice grew bitter. "Dee Vernor, the original hick from the colonies. I was a complete misfit, and worse" — she spread her hands in a gesture of despair — "I still don't know where I belong!"

Morgan placed her arm around her. "Dee, I meant it about the Academy. It isn't important. All that any of us care about now is your happiness." She squeezed a thin shoulder. "You know, I've wondered if you shouldn't have gone into veterinary studies. Remember the menageries you always had when you were little? The mice and the fish, and that sick kissat you nursed? And what about the sorkka you tamed?"

"Yes, they were special to me. But I don't know what I want to do with my life. In fact, right now I feel as if I don't want to do anything at all. As if I'm caught in some sort of a trap and *can't* do anything. Does that make sense to you?"

"I think so. You *have* been sick, no matter what the doctors say. You need to rest and get your strength back and not worry about what comes next."

Dee leaned her head against Morgan's shoulder. "You do understand! If only Daddy —"

"He will, too." Morgan gave her a hug and got up. "You know how much he loves you." She wanted to spend more time with Dee, but a glance at her watch confirmed that she couldn't. She had appointments all morning, and even if she left now she would be late for the first one.

Arnie agreed that she could take the flitter. He and Dee would manage on the bus, he said. Reminding him of his final promise to keep her posted, Morgan dashed up the outside stairs to the roof pad.

Over the city, she had smooth currents and an unobstructed path. Usually she was able to leave her home problems behind, but not this morning. She could think of nothing but Dee, and these worries served no purpose and would surely hamper her efficiency if she took them to work.

She turned to a mental discipline she sometimes practiced, breathing in and out with a favorite mantra. It worked, clearing her mind and allowing her to realax. When she landed on the SEF pad she was once again Farraday, the school superintendent.

Morgan's first appointment, a reporter from the *Friishaven Herald,* was waiting in the anteroom. "Here, better read this before I show him in," Jazmin said. She handed Morgan a red-flagged memo.

It was signed by Commander Nurmi. "SEF personnel are to refrain from publicly expressing any opinion regarding the proposed Argus Two," it stated. "SEF has formulated no official policy, and employees must under no circumstances jeopardize this neutrality."

Neutral! That certainly wasn't the impression Morgan had received yesterday. And she had no time for a crash course in Nurmi-style diplomacy: the press interview was *now.*

She expressed her misgivings to Jazmin.

"Hey, don't worry. You have a ready-made answer," Jazmin said. "If he mentions Argus Two, just smile and tell him you're too new to Jaspre to have formed any opinions. Are you ready now? That's one impatient reporter. He's about to wear out the carpet."

"I'm as ready as I'll ever be." Morgan seated herself behind her desk and jotted quick notes on possible school improvements to bring up. Still nervous, she reached for a stack of printouts, shuffled them, and stacked them.

The young man had the flat nose and carroty hair she had seen in many of the Friislanders. He wore black workman's coveralls and an unfriendly scowl.

Morgan rose and held out her hand. "I'm Morgan Farraday. Won't you —"

He ignored her, setting up holo equipment and half

blinding her with a light flash. When he finally held out his own hand, his shake was perfunctory.

"You're not what I expected to see," he said. "Are you sure this is the right office? Our new school supervisor? Maybe I've stumbled into a modeling agency instead." For all the surface flattery, his tone was cynical, as was his appraising stare as he continued: "Is there a special school for administrators now, to do away with all those boring years of experience?"

Morgan held back hot words. If he was trying to get a story by riling her, he would be disappointed. "No, I got my post in the usual fashion," she said. "I've served on more worlds than you could guess." She tried a disarming smile. "I've always wanted to see Jaspre, and I can't tell you how pleased I am to be here."

The tactic had no effect; he continued to frown. "Do you really believe you can understand the educational needs of children on a world you haven't even visited before?"

"SEF does," Morgan answered. "Space Corps teachers and supervisors are regularly rotated to give them as varied experiences as possible."

"But each situation is unique, isn't it? Wouldn't it be better, especially in an administrator, to have someone who is familiar with the peculiar problems of his or her region?"

She clutched a pencil in tight fingers. "We're concerned with matters of literacy. They're pretty universal. And the Space Corps sends teachers only where they're requested."

"Requested by whom? On Jaspre, I mean."

"Jaspre is a colonial planet. SEF knows its needs."

"Better than the colonists themselves?"

45

He certainly was out for her blood. An independence crusader, and there was no way she could satisfy him. "Why don't you wait, before you judge me? I don't propose to make any reforms until I'm thoroughly familiar with the schools. The first thing I'm planning is a series of visits."

"Visits. Yes. To Space Corps schools and Space Corps teachers. A lot you're likely to learn about the needs of Jaspre."

"So what would you suggest?" Besides my resignation, she thought.

He eyed her narrowly. "Are you serious?"

She nodded, trying to keep the tension from her face. He could damage her position badly, with the story she knew he intended.

"Then you might begin by attending a citizens' rally we're holding tonight. It's to demand information about Argus Two. As much as Commander Nurmi says he values our opinion, he's tried his best to keep us from knowing anything about this latest brainstorm."

Morgan swallowed. "I meant school needs," she said. "I really don't think . . . the other . . . is pertinent."

The redhead barked a laugh. "I thought you'd say that. No, melting glaciers and flooding half a continent has nothing to do with children or their future. Nothing to do with you, anyway. You'll be safely gone, collecting more 'varied experiences.'" He stood up. "Thank you for your time. I think I have my story."

Morgan remained slumped in her chair. He would flay her. And ironically, she sympathized with his position, though she could never say so. She crumpled her notepad with all the ideas she hadn't been allowed to present. If only she were still a teacher, she thought, with no problems beyond the classroom.

"Hey, why the long face? It couldn't have gone that badly." Jazmin came in with more printouts. "The bookspool inventory you ordered. You have half an hour before the curriculum committee is due. Want to go through it now?"

Morgan shook her head. "I'm going up for some fresh air."

She ran into Justin DiVoto on the roof terrace. "I dropped by your office," he said. "That dragon guard of yours wouldn't let me in."

"I had a meeting. A press interview."

"How did it go?"

"Terribly." She considered: If Justin was sincere about his offer to help, she could use some advice.

She related the disaster. "When that interview gets printed, Commander Nurmi will have a fit. I hate to think what he'll say to me."

"You *are* worried, aren't you? Don't give it a thought. The *Herald* is notoriously biased against SEF. As far as our boss is concerned, he'd only react if they printed anything flattering, it would be so unusual."

Relief flooded her. "I thought that reporter had it in for me personally. He certainly didn't think I was fit for my job."

"He wouldn't, but it has nothing to do with you. It's this damned Argus Two leak. Everyone on the planet knows about it now. Apparently they have for weeks. The *Herald* is a muckraking rag that takes the snowgrubbers' view of Argus Two, and according to both of them, anyone connected with SEF is a villain."

"Snowgrubbers?"

"It's what we call the Lumislanders. Those nuts out on the ice living on visions and puerhu blubber. For some reason they like their life and don't want it to change, and some Friislanders have adopted their cause."

"What about the danger to Friisland itself? The floods?"

He tensed. "I told you, forget what that reporter says. Argus Two will cause only minor inconveniences. The engineers have it all figured. You heard the report. The amount of coast we'll lose is negligible."

"And the difference in climate? What about the farmers?"

"They can change crops. If they don't want to do that, they can move to Lumisland. That continent will be able to support thousands. Millions, eventually. The snowgrubbers could go farther north, if they really wanted that kind of life. Or if they're crazy enough, down to that howling wasteland in the southern zone. There'll be plenty of options for them."

Justin's view sounded reasonable. Still, the citizens of Jaspre apparently didn't buy it. Why wouldn't Nurmi even listen to them?

Justin seemed to read her mind. "Where would SEF be if we let all of our planets dictate their own policies? It would be chaos — maybe even war. No, we have to maintain control, for the protection of Earth.

"In this case, we're taking the long view — what's really best for Jaspre — while those 'No on Two' groups are wearing blinders. You can see that, can't you?"

Morgan nodded, though she was not entirely convinced. Still, she returned to her office feeling better about the interview.

The curriculum meeting went smoothly. Afterward, she returned a call from Arnie.

"We just got back from the hospital," he said. "Dee's fine. The doctors couldn't find any physical problem. There are test results to come, but it looks good." He grimaced. "They think she should go in for psychiatric counseling."

Morgan could see that Arnie resisted the idea. "Why not?" she asked.

"I don't see the point. Dee's not ill *that* way. I know it. She's always been such a joy."

"Maybe that's part of her problem," Morgan said. "Maybe it's been too hard for her, being considered so perfect."

"I don't know what you mean."

Morgan sighed. "You will agree to the counseling, though?"

"Sure. What do I know — I'm only her father. But I'm also going to look for a tutor for her. Maybe Dee can still get back into the Academy, when she's better."

"If she wants to." Morgan didn't tell Arnie that she had been thinking of something quite different for Dee. Couldn't her affinity for animals be both useful and healing? Morgan pictured Dee and the twin-horned sorkka she had tamed on New Terra, the skittish creature eating out of the girl's hand.

As soon as she touched off from Arnie, she called the

Friishaven Zoological Institute and was assured that they could use a trainee. At least Dee could have that option, if Arnie pressed too hard.

And he would press. Arnie wasn't one to give up easily. If only Dee could have the backbone to stand up to him.

Anxious, Morgan hurried through her most pressing tasks and left for home early, only to find when she got there that Dee had gone out sightseeing with Matt.

They returned in grumpy silence. Matt had wanted to go down to the harbor to watch the fishing boats come in, but they had run into an anti–Argus Two demonstration and Dee had insisted on returning home. "There were about a dozen people, waving dinky signs," Matt said with disgust. "There wasn't a thing to be afraid of."

Dee said nothing, but her white face and the line between her brows proclaimed another headache. She murmured an excuse and went to her room.

"I wanted to talk to her about the tutor," Arnie said.

"Let it wait a while," Morgan advised. At least, she thought, until she could make her own suggestion.

Arnie had prepared a special welcome-home dinner, and Dee joined them at the table. She apologized to Matt and assured Morgan and Arnie that she was fine, but Morgan didn't believe it.

Arnie apparently did. He urged food on Dee and beamed when she forced it down. He even suggested that they all go together the next night to the mayor's ball, a function he had previously complained about attending.

To Morgan's surprise, Dee agreed.

"It's okay, I can handle it," she insisted when Morgan

spoke to her later, alone. "I have to learn to tolerate crowds, and I might as well start now. This afternoon with Matt — all those people shouting — it was like Earth, and I panicked. I shouldn't have given in."

"Arnie spoke to you about the psychiatrist?"

"Yes. I'm willing to see anyone, if it will help me. I hate it, the way I am. So silly and weak, and no use to anyone." The wide, violet eyes misted with tears, and Morgan had to steel herself to keep from crying, too.

Later, when Arnie said how much better he felt about Dee, Morgan wondered how he could be so blind.

✳3✳

Dee borrowed a gown of Morgan's for the mayor's ball. It was creamy off-white, long and gauzy and freeflowing enough to hide the sharpness of her bones. She wore her cornsilk hair loose, and with a pearly touch of color to her cheeks, she had an ethereal beauty.

Morgan chose a simple tunic and sleek, fitted pants of dark Midian silk. After the interview that had appeared in the *Herald,* she wanted only to escape notice.

She couldn't get it out of her mind. When she gave a final touch to her hair, instead of her reflection in the glass she saw the news photo of a blowzy, bug-eyed woman with her mouth hanging open. "SEF Picks New Terran to Run Schools," the headline had read. Out-of-context quotes had made her sound as much a fool as the photo suggested: an empty-headed adventuress totally unconcerned with the welfare of Jaspre.

If it had been possible, she would have begged off appearing tonight. No one at SEF had mentioned the article, but Morgan feared that the Friishaven townspeople might not be as polite.

Arnie and Matt came into the bedroom, shining in silver formal wear. Arnie wore his service medals, and Matt a bit of the ribbon. "How do I look?" Matt asked. His eyes were as bright as his costume.

"As handsome as your father," Morgan said. "Now remember: no running around, no snitching food until it's offered, and no punch of any kind. Lord knows what they'll put into it."

"Aw, Mom. I know how to act."

Arnie tousled the boy's hair. "Then see that you do it. I remember a certain reception on New Terra. As far as I'm concerned, young man, you're still on party probation."

"I'll take him home after he's had his chance at the food," Dee said. She stood in the doorway, fastening her cloak. "That's all he's interested in, and I don't want to stay late, either."

"No dancing?" Morgan asked. Dee used to love it.

"At least once, with your old man," Arnie said.

Dee smiled and took his arm.

The city hall, a round building with a traditional rotunda, was ablaze with lights. Spectators thronged the canopied entrance, forcing the invited guests to walk a gauntlet of stares and comments. Half of Friishaven must be here, Morgan thought as they joined the crush waiting to be admitted.

Inside it was better, with the guests spreading through the domed central hall and four adjoining rooms. Dee held tightly to Arnie's arm as they moved toward the receiving line. She looked edgy, but Morgan had to trust her to Arnie; keeping track of Matt took all of her attention. She lost the boy once, found him again, and maintained a tight grip on his shoulder as the introductions began.

The dignitaries were beribboned and bejeweled: the mayor and his wife, the council members and their spouses, a representative from West Region, Commander and Mrs. Nurmi, and attending them, Justin DiVoto.

Morgan introduced her family. "My son, Matthew Vernor. Arnie I think you know. My daughter, Delila Vernor."

Dee floated up to Justin, angelically. "Delila," he murmured. He held her hand considerably longer than necessary.

"Dee," the angel said, giggling.

They were through the line and faced with long tables of decoratively arranged food. A band played on the rotunda stairs, and couples were beginning to dance.

"Shall we try it?" Arnie asked.

"I'd better keep an eye on Matt," Morgan said. The boy had a plate piled high with pastries. "You go ahead and dance with Dee."

"It's too late."

Morgan followed Arnie's gaze to the white-clad figure swaying gracefully in Justin's arms. Justin's place by Commander Nurmi had been taken by another officer, and the receiving line was beginning to break up.

"Our new school chief, isn't it? I thought I recognized you from the news photo."

Morgan struggled to remember the name; it was one of the council members to whom she had just been introduced.

It came to her. "Mr. Orm. Yes, but I wish you hadn't. Such an awful picture."

"Unflattering, I see now. But the article . . . Do you really intend to restructure our schools to the pattern of some other planet?"

"No, I didn't say that at all. I only thought my experience might be useful."

"Mara was terribly upset." Orm drew his wife into the group.

"Every few years it's someone new, meddling with the schools," Mara Orm said. "The teachers, too. As soon as they begin to learn our ways, they're sent off somewhere else."

Jaspre couldn't be too far from training its own teachers, Morgan thought. Perhaps she should suggest that they speed up the process. She didn't say it, however; not with the room so liberally sprinkled with SEF uniforms.

The circle around Morgan grew larger. "Do you really look upon your appointment here as nothing more than an 'exciting adventure'?"

"Do you really consider yourself qualified?"

She tried to answer, but her interrogators wouldn't listen. Then she saw Dee signaling from across the floor, excused herself, and broke free.

Perspiration beaded Dee's brow. "The noise," she said. "I feel suffocated. If you can find Matt, Justin has offered to take us home in his flitter."

"Dee is still suffering a reaction from the jumps," Justin said. "She shouldn't be exposed to crowds until she's gotten her land legs." The look he gave Morgan was accusing.

55

"I'll get Matt," Morgan said.

Matt had eaten his fill and came willingly. Justin had their wraps and helped Dee into her cloak as carefully as if she were made of fragile glass. "I can't believe she's your daughter," he said to Morgan.

Morgan wondered whether she should take it as a compliment or an insult. Probably it was meant as neither, she decided; Justin was too entranced by Dee to have any other thoughts.

The three left, and Morgan rejoined Arnie. He had filled a plate for her, and they moved well away from the group around Councilor Orm.

"Excuse me, but aren't you —" Another irate citizen bore down upon her.

"No, I . . . you're mistaken; I don't believe I know you," Morgan stammered. She put down her plate and whispered to Arnie, "Let's go."

"I'll get the coats," Arnie said. Morgan saw Mara Orm looking her way, and headed for the coatroom herself.

A commotion at the main entrance drew her up short. Two civilian guards pushed past as they hurried to investigate.

Voices grew louder as the guards and the door attendants tried vainly to hold back a phalanx of gatecrashers.

A mob of them erupted into the main hall, shouting and waving signs. NO ARGUS TWO. JASPRE FOR JASPRIANS. Bold letters and angry voices and clenched fists.

Arnie appeared and pulled Morgan against a wall. "No, I want to see," she said and moved out again.

The intruders had found and encircled the mayor and

Commander Nurmi. There was too much noise for Morgan to hear what was going on, but someone near her said something about presenting petitions.

Morgan caught a glimpse of the mayor's crimson face. Commander Nurmi shouldered his way out of the circle, and no one stopped him.

The demonstrators filed out without making any more trouble. By their dress they appeared to be Friisland farmers and laborers, but a conspicuous handful wore the thick woolens and furs of a harsher climate.

"Snowgrubbers," Morgan heard. As they passed her, she studied the dark, leathery faces with interest. Their eyes were slits beneath heavy epicanthic folds. The one gaze she met was piercing and strangely unsettling.

"It's over," Arnie said. "Let's get out now, before your fans find you again."

"I think they've forgotten me," Morgan assured him. Around her, everyone was discussing the intrusion and the appearance of the snowgrubbers.

Morgan would have liked to stay and listen, but Arnie continued to urge her to the door. "I don't feel right about Dee. You shouldn't have let her go off with that tin soldier DiVoto. How well do you know him?"

"Arnie! Matt is with them. And Dee isn't a child anymore!"

Arnie grinned sheepishly.

At home, Dee and Matt were both in bed. "I'm still going to check that guy out," Arnie said. "If he's going to be hanging around Dee, I want to know all about him. You can't be too careful."

Arnie lost no time carrying out his promise. When he had obtained his information, he had to admit that Justin's credentials were more than satisfactory.

"Actually, Dee couldn't do much better," he reported. He and Matt and Morgan were perched on boulders in the back yard, watching the men from Green Growers roll out their new lawn. Dee had gone with Justin for a countryside flyover and picnic. "The young man's steady as a rock," Arnie continued. "And he's crazy about Dee."

"You amaze me!" Morgan was half joking, half serious as she threw up her hands. "First you do an about-face on Justin, and now it's Dee. Yesterday you wanted her back in the Academy, and today you're ready to marry her off."

Arnie ignored the teasing. "I had a long talk with Justin before they left. He knows how . . . unsettled . . . Dee is, and he promised to look after her. I trust him."

"You should. He wouldn't dare do anything to jeopardize his position as the commander's fair-haired boy."

Morgan's irony was lost on Arnie. "He has a good future," he said soberly. "And Dee seems to like him."

Matt scuffed his foot in the border of newly laid soil. "Dee's really got the space bejeebers," he said. "Did I tell you that when we went to the harbor together, she was afraid to even cross the streets?"

"No, but you should have," Morgan said.

"Don't talk about it outside the family," Arnie warned. "It's nobody else's business."

The lawn lay smooth and flat as a square of green carpet. "I'll scatter some wildflower seeds," Morgan said. "It could use some weeds, too."

"We need trees," Arnie said. He went to talk to the workmen.

"When are we going to the snow country?" Matt asked. "The *real* Jaspre?"

"As soon as I can manage," Morgan said.

Argus passed in front of the sun, and for a few moments there was a perceptible cooling. Then the two orbs appeared as a single brilliant oval that gradually elongated itself into a searing band of light.

"At least I have Arnie and Matt and Dee," Morgan said to Jazmin as she hung up her coat Monday morning. "I don't know what I'd do without their support. Everyone in town recognizes me now — public enemy number one! Things couldn't get much worse."

"I hope not," Jazmin said.

Something in her tone alerted Morgan. "What is it? What do you know?"

Jazmin's face was expressionless. Perhaps too much so. "Commander Nurmi wants to see you. Right away."

Morgan clutched the rail tightly as she climbed the stairs.

As usual, the commander was succinct. "There's an East Region school in Lumisland, isn't there?" he asked.

Morgan nodded. "One." She hadn't even been invited to sit.

"Then get ready to go there for an inspection. Immediately. Tomorrow at the latest. After that you can set up an office in the town, Lumisatama, and conduct whatever school business you have from there. Until further notice."

He waved aside her questions. "Lieutenant DiVoto will

give you the details." He stood up to dismiss her, and she left in total confusion.

Justin was waiting in the outer office. Morgan sank into the chair he offered and clasped her trembling knees. "Why? I don't understand. What does it mean?"

He brought her a cup of water. "Take it easy."

"Go ahead, tell me. Why am I being shipped out?"

"Public relations. Starting at the mayor's party, and all weekend, the commander's been bombarded with complaints about your appointment. From everyone who read that mucky interview and believed what it seemed to say."

"But you said he wouldn't pay any attention to it."

"Ordinarily he wouldn't have. But now that he's getting all this flak about Argus Two, he can't afford to arouse any more animosity."

"And you told me not to worry!"

Justin looked momentarily contrite. "I know, and I'm really sorry. But I didn't anticipate the reaction, either. It's all part of their damned independence movement. SEF has to placate the Jasprians, and since they've taken up your case as an example of our poor judgment, we can't do anything while you're so visible."

"So I'm to be kept out of sight. For how long?"

"Until things cool down. Or until we get the go-ahead from Earth on Argus Two. It'll be too late then for protests."

There seemed to be no use arguing. Morgan moved to the next problem. "But my job. Am I really expected to run the schools from Lumisland?"

"Why not? You can be in communication with us here by mail and by radio phone."

"Radio! Is it that primitive?"

"Yes, it is. But you may be thankful for the isolation. At least your bad press won't follow you there."

He was so matter-of-fact about it all. No hint of sympathy. "Aren't you the least bit concerned about sending me out to the snowgrubbers?"

"You're a strong woman, Morgan. You'll be fine."

He made her feel like an Amazon prizefighter.

"Now, Dee . . ." His face softened into an expression of tenderness. "I wouldn't advise her even visiting you there. Not until she's regained her strength."

"Perhaps I shouldn't leave her." Let him squirm some.

"Oh, no! She'll be in good hands. Arnie and I —"

"I expect that Arnie will be with me soon."

"Then I'll make Dee my responsibility. I've already promised to take her to the hospital this afternoon, for her appointment with the psychiatrist. Not that I think she needs one. There's nothing wrong with Dee but overstrain, from her Academy load." He frowned. "She should never have been encouraged to enroll there. It's no place for someone like her, someone so delicate and sensitive."

He was so infuriatingly cocksure. And the nerve, going along with Nurmi and shipping her off like a piece of bad equipment! Probably he hadn't even voiced an objection. She had wanted to see the snow country, but not this way!

She exploded. "So I'm not to worry about Dee, eh? You think it's that easy? And Arnie and Matt, what are they supposed to do? Arnie's still looking for work, and Matt has just started school. And there's the house. We signed a lease, and we can't afford to rent two places!"

Her voice rose until it broke in a squeak. "Tomorrow! The commander said I was to leave tomorrow. Is he out of his mind?"

Justin ignored the note of hysteria. "I'm to have a SEF tachjet ready for you in the morning. Say, seven o'clock?"

"Do I have a choice?"

"Not if you want to keep your job."

He had her there. She arose stiffly. "I'll be ready."

"You'll have the regular travel allowance, for as long as you're away," he said in a conciliatory tone. "It'll go a long way in Lumisland. You'll be okay financially."

"Yes. As you said, I'll be fine." She held her back straight as she marched out.

Jazmin helped her to pack a carrycase. "It may not be for long," the secretary said, but Morgan doubted that she would be returning to the cramped little office. What kind of a cubbyhole would she have in Lumisatama? she wondered. Maybe an igloo.

"Lumisatama," she said aloud. "What sort of a name is that, anyway?"

Jazmin shrugged. "A snowgrubber word. You'll hear lots of them up there."

"Have you been there?"

"Once, to see the snows. It was beautiful, but I didn't stay long."

Morgan didn't ask why. She had enough to worry about, preparing to leave on such short notice. She gave Jazmin what instructions she could, mostly to stand by for radioed dispatches, and left to give Arnie the bad news.

He was as dismayed as she had expected. "If I'd known what we'd be faced with here . . . Why did I ever let you talk us into leaving New Terra?" He slammed his fist into his palms and muttered curses. "Does Nurmi expect us to pack up and follow you?"

"I don't think he cares. Just so he's rid of me."

"I can't go now. Even with no job to keep me, with Dee the way she is . . . We can't leave Matt with her."

"I know. But maybe in a week or so, when I've had a chance to scout out living accommodations, you can all come for a visit. We'll just have to see how it goes."

They left it at that. Morgan continued to grumble along with Arnie as they packed and sorted, the more so to hide a spark of excitement that had ignited in spite of the circumstances. The snows, she thought . . .

✳4✳

The plane headed due north over the ocean. Feathery whitecaps dotted the slate blue surface until streaks of clouds intervened. Then they were above the clouds in a gray void of silent motion.

Morgan was the only passenger. She supposed she should feel important, but instead she was embarrassed by the extravagance of the empty seats around her.

She closed her eyes. Guilt: it seemed to be stalking her. She had been too keyed up to sleep the previous night, her mood swinging wildly from anticipation to remorse. It was the worst possible time to be leaving, with Dee lost and vulnerable, while Morgan was on her way to fulfill a dream. *The snows. The colored snows.* The words rang echoing in her mind like Praxian soundbeads, with a corresponding vision of cold, flashing beauty.

A voice shattered her reverie. "You must be some VIP to rate this service." A pause. "Oh, I'm sorry. I didn't see that you were sleeping." Morgan opened her eyes as the junior pilot began to back out of the passenger compartment.

"It's all right, I wasn't," she said quickly. She smiled and patted the adjoining seat. "And I'm a VIP only as far as it's very important for Commander Nurmi to get rid of me in such a hurry that he couldn't wait for a commercial flight."

"Funny, you don't look dangerous. And we're not drawing hazard pay." The young man slid into the seat. He had reddish hair and a distinct Friisland cast to his features.

Morgan's curiosity was piqued; she could remember seeing few Friislanders in Force uniforms. "I thought you people hated SEF."

"Not all of us." He removed his cap and placed it carefully across a knee. He looked very young and very earnest. "Sure, I'd like nothing better than to see Jaspre with its own space force. But I couldn't wait for that to happen, not if I wanted to fly before I was too old to qualify."

"If you can't beat 'em —"

He grinned. "That's what I figured."

"Lucky for us. And I'm glad you came back to talk to me. Maybe you can give me some information about this place I'm being exiled to."

"If I can."

"I'm curious about the names. Lumisland. Lumisatama. Does it have anything to do with Argus light?"

He shook his head. "That's what most people think, but the names were here before SEF put up Argus. Lumisland means snowland, and Lumisatama means snow harbor or snow port. Usually the settlers just call it Satama.

"It's one of the old Earth languages. The original settlers

on Jaspre were Lapland Finns, dispossessed by the Northern Wars. Jaspre was only borderline habitable then, in a narrow band at the equator. It was a hard life, but those snowgrubbers managed to survive by reverting to old ways. They had a quality they call *sisu,* a sort of stubborn tenacity that they take pride in yet today. When Argus went up, they moved to a new Lumisland, and they're still dug in there. The most ornery, bullheaded bunch of cusses you'd ever be unlucky enough to meet."

"Why do I get the feeling, then, that you admire them?"

"Maybe I do. The old-time grubbers, anyway. They mind their own business and only want to be left alone. It's Anders Ahlwen and his bunch that are causing all the trouble. No one wants to get mixed up with *them.*"

"Why not?"

He shifted uneasily. "Crackpots. Snow's got to them. You'll hear. There's talk enough in Satama." He replaced his cap, positioning it exactly with both hands. "I ought to go back up front now. Why don't you catch a nap? I'll let you know when we start our descent, as soon as there's something to see."

Morgan did sleep finally, and the intercom awakened her to another world. They were below the clouds, making a great circle over the east coast of Lumisland. Argus and the real sun were both low on the southern horizon, but they were too close together for it to be much past noon. The real sun was a fuzzy, reddish brown glow that Morgan could barely see, but Argus stained the sky with all the colors of sunset, and they were reflected off the sharp-edged icebergs

66

that studded the dark water like the tips of jeweled mountains.

Through the left viewport Morgan could see a glistening mass of snow and ice, splashed with a shifting kaleidoscope of colors. Patterns emerged and then shaded into others: blood red to soft rose to mauve to the whole spectrum of blues, thin spears of yellow-gold and soft washes of green, a rainbow palette.

"This is the best view you can get of Argus light," said a voice from the speaker. "We overflew a bit to give it to you."

The colorful snow plain retreated as the jet turned to follow a barren, rocky coastline. They continued to descend over a landlocked harbor and a town that huddled at the base of dark mountains, treeless and naked except for colored caps of snow.

The landing field was well beyond the town. Morgan climbed down the ramp into a cold that penetrated her jacket and pants, instantly chilling her to the bone.

"Over there, ma'am." The younger pilot pointed her toward a shedlike building. "Wait in there. The crawler'll be along to take you into town."

She clenched her teeth and bent into the wind. The dirty gray slush that covered the tarmac promised havoc to her dress boots. She tried at first to avoid the deeper patches but gave up when she felt the wet soak through.

Uniform be damned! The pilots, she had noticed, had changed to arctic gear to help unload. She felt like a bad joke in her spit-and-polish.

At least she could get more comfortable. Inside the drafty terminal, Morgan fished in her duffel for a pair of padded pants and a thick sweater. She pulled them on over her other clothes and followed them with a knitted cap and mittens.

The crawler, a ground bus with balloon tires, arrived, and the driver hopped out. "You're for Satama?" She helped Morgan with her gear, then drove across the landing field to collect the cargo crates from the plane.

"Good luck," the redheaded pilot called.

"Aren't they stopping over?" Morgan asked her driver.

"Nope. The weather's good, and who'd risk getting stuck in this dump?"

Morgan's sinking spirits took another dive. "Why? What's so terrible about it?"

The woman, sturdy and gray-haired, with a broad, ruddy face, laughed without humor. "Look around you."

They were heading toward the harbor and the town along a road that was nothing more than a mud track. A sleety gray drizzle had begun to fall. Argus was obscured by a bank of fog, and the dirty snow that was piled in half-melted banks on either side of the road reflected no colors. Toward the ocean stretched gravel pits and forbidding black rock formations, and to the mountains a desolate waste of frozen furzee. The surface of the ocean, when Morgan glimpsed it between the rocks, was a dead black, broken by enormous gray ice floes that damped the motion of the waves.

The driver read Morgan's face. "Disappointed? Everyone is when they land here. Satama's the rats' end of Jaspre, but it's the only way you can get in to the snows." She looked at Morgan again more sharply. "But you're no tourist, coming in on a SEF plane. What brings you to our little paradise?"

"Business. I'll probably be here a while."

"Congratulations! You couldn't have picked a more charming spot!"

The woman's cynicism began to grate on Morgan. "If you hate it so much here, why do you stay?"

She tightened her mouth to a grim line. "Anders Ahlwen."

"That name again."

"So you've heard of him? I'm not surprised. He must be cursed by now, all the way to Friishaven."

"No. I mean I've heard the name, but only from the pilot on the plane. But then, I'm new to Jaspre. What has this Ahlwen done?"

The woman spun the wheel on a curve and sent a sheet of frozen slush flying. "You want to know? Ask anyone."

"I'm asking you."

"I wish you hadn't." She grimaced again and then shrugged. "Well, you might as well hear it from me as long as you're staying here. There are a lot of folks who've got it in for Ahlwen, and I'm no exception. That renegade grubber's got my . . . a friend of mine . . . in one of those underground camps of his. I'm not leaving this frozen hell until I get her out of there."

"You mean she's been kidnapped?"

"As far as I'm concerned, she has. They won't let me in to see her, so how do I know what's going on?"

It seemed to be all she was willing to say, and Morgan

did not press. Through the window the countryside continued, scoured by the bleakness and the cold. The furze tundra was despoiled now with great gouges filled with black water and cores of ice. They passed the first person Morgan had seen since leaving the airport, a well-bundled man carrying a large shovel. A groundsled loaded with squares of furze turf followed him, heading for a long row of dilapidated buildings covered with permafiber sheeting.

"Furze-drying sheds," the driver said. "Along with the fish and the tourists, it's what keeps the town going."

The town proper, in the shadow of the mountain, consisted of a cannery by the harbor and half a dozen weathered buildings along the one street. Morgan spotted a store, a bar, and what looked like a heavy-equipment garage. A structure with a bell hanging from its porch roof she guessed to be the school.

"You want the lodge, don't you?" the driver asked. Morgan nodded, and they drove up to a steep track with switchbacks, past smaller houses built of stone or patched together from scraps of metal and woodplas. There was snow here, but the dull gray light that bathed the landscape did not transform it.

The lodge was a rambling stone structure that appeared to grow out of the mountain. "I'm staying here, too," the driver said. "So we'll be seeing each other." She swung the crawler expertly around the entry curve, parked, and extended her hand. "I'm Elsie Tersteegen."

"Morgan Farraday."

Elsie helped with the bags and left Morgan at the front door. "I'll see you at dinner," she said.

"I'll look for you," Morgan answered. The woman's story intrigued her, and she hoped to hear more of it. She watched the driver lumber off in her thick boots and bulky quilted coverall. An unlikely figure for a rescuing knight. Yet there had been that dogged determination . . .

The lodge entry hall was bare and drafty, with a ski rack near the door and an assortment of wraps hanging on pegs. Morgan rang a bell at the reception desk and waited.

A brown-faced sprite with the droopy eyelids of a snowgrubber appeared. "You must be the school inspector," she said. "We've been expecting you. Come in here and get warm." She led the way to a sitting room furnished with sturdy chairs and bright woven hangings on the walls. A fire crackled in an open fireplace. "I'll get Dad," she said, and left Morgan to thaw.

Dad turned out to be Magnus Borstrup, the manager, a tall, thin man with a shock of gray-streaked hair and pale blue grubber eyes under bushy eyebrows. Morgan bargained a bit, since it seemed to be expected, and finally engaged a room and meals for an indefinite period. The rates were low, and there would be no difficulty in accommodating Arnie and Matt and Dee.

The room was spartan: a bed, a chair, and a dresser; a curtained closet; and a bathroom down the hall. Borstrup promised to bring in a table, though he suggested that she would be more comfortable doing whatever paperwork she had in the downstairs sitting room. Morgan felt the heating grate, which was barely warm, and agreed.

She unpacked, changed into thermal underwear, soft knits, and dry boots, and made her way downstairs again. She

71

placed a call to Arnie on the radio phone in Borstrup's office but failed to reach him.

The lodge appeared to be empty. Morgan peeked into the dining room, where the manager's daughter was laying the tables. She saw Morgan and looked up. "Dinner's at five," she said. "So there's time for skiing after. That's when it's best."

"I'd like to go," Morgan said, "but I don't have the clothes or gear."

"We can fix you up." She was older than Morgan had first thought, a small-boned teenager, not a child.

Morgan introduced herself.

"Karla Borstrup," the girl said with a ducking curtsy. She was dressed in a woolen skirt and vest, bright with embroidery. Her eyes were the same pale blue as her father's.

Another maid came in, wearing a similar costume. Karla moved to join her, and Morgan left them whispering together.

She found a reader and a box of bookspools in the sitting room and curled up in a cushioned chair. She read until Karla called her for dinner.

There were ten guests in the dining room: a noisy party of skiers exhilarated by their day on the snows, two solitary diners at individual tables, and Elsie and Morgan at a table for two. Karla and her friend served fish stew, much too salty, with gluey vegetables that obviously came from a packet. The freshly baked bread, however, was delicious.

"I've been here six months now," Elsie said in answer to a question of Morgan's. "Driving the crawler pays for my keep, but Britt and I both lost good jobs in Friishaven. And that's on Ahlwen's head, too." Her brows met in a glowering scowl. "You want to know about him? There's plenty to tell, and none of it good. He's a soul-sucking monster masquerading as a man, and if someone doesn't shoot him soon he'll have corrupted half of Lumisland." She whacked the table with her fist, and her voice boomed. "And what do the authorities do? SEF and that lily-livered bunch of so-called snow patrols? Nothing! While every day more deluded pigeons disappear into those holes he calls camps and are never seen again." She was off on a tirade, attracting stares from all the tables.

"Tell me about Britt," Morgan said softly, to subdue her and get her back on track.

Elsie heaved a sigh and, after a moment of silence, proceeded more calmly. "We'd gone for the skiing, Britt and I. It was our first trip to the snows. We'd been planning it for ages, but somehow we could never work out our schedules. But finally it came together, and we were here, and Britt was . . . transported . . . by all the beauty. You'll see, when you go out. No one expects it, no matter what they've heard. Britt is an artist, and it affected her more than most. Then she had an accident — nothing serious, just a sprain — while we were trekking to First Station Lodge, and the grubber who found us was one of them — one of Ahlwen's toadies.

"He had a sled and he took us both to their camp, which wasn't far. About fifteen miles north and east. They wouldn't let us stay together, and the next day they told me that Britt didn't want to leave."

"Didn't you see her?"

"Just for a few minutes. She told me to go away, and I

was so furious with her then that I hightailed it right out of there. But now when I think back on it I know she wasn't in her right mind. They did something to her, and I'll never rest until I get her out of that madman's clutches."

"Whatever you think of him, he's not a madman." Karla Borstrup, clearing the table, raised her chin defiantly. "I saw Anders Ahlwen once, at Second Station Lodge. He was giving a talk, and what he said made sense to me. I've felt the power in the snow, lots of times, and I felt it in him. People hate him because they're afraid of him, or they're jealous because he has something they haven't."

"Something . . . like what?" Morgan asked.

"Karla!" shouted her father from the kitchen. Karla jumped and finished wiping the spills. She loaded her tray and moved to the next table.

"What did she mean about the power?" Morgan asked Elsie.

The big woman snorted. "Some mystical nonsense about the Argus-lit snow. Absolute rubbish, but it appeals to a lot of soft-minded people. Especially the young; you know how impressionable they are."

"Britt isn't young," Karla said over her shoulder.

Elsie glared. "She's like a baby in some ways. She was always too trusting."

"What kind of powers?" Morgan asked again, this time of Karla.

"Mine-expanding," the girl said. "But you have to be on the snows a long time for it to work on you. You have to make the journey."

"Karla, that's enough!" Borstrup made a threatening motion.

Karla hurried off with her tray.

Elsie stared into her mug of coffee. "I know she didn't really want me to leave her," she said.

"You've gone back for her since?" Morgan prompted.

"Many times. His guards won't let me in." She looked up at Morgan with moist eyes. "Would you like to go with me, to see for yourself? Maybe somebody new — a stranger — would have more luck. Please. I haven't gotten anywhere alone."

Why not? Morgan thought. Her time would hang heavy here, and she felt sorry for Elsie. "Yes, I'll go," she said. "I thought I'd visit the school tomorrow. That's why I'm here, you know. I'm with the Space Corps. But after that —"

"It suits me fine. The day after tomorrow's my day off, too. Are you any good on skis?"

"It's been a while. But yes, I think I can manage."

"So you're connected with the schools. Why didn't you tell me before? I wouldn't have shot off my mouth about SEF. Anyway, you can meet the teacher right now. That's her over there."

Elsie pointed to one of the solitary diners, a pretty young woman with large, soft features and a bush of wiry black hair. She had her attention fixed on the screen of a pocket-sized reader while she ate her dessert. When she rose and prepared to leave, Elsie waved.

The teacher stopped at their table, and Elsie made the introductions. Arin Molino blinked nervously as she stared down at Morgan. "I . . . certainly wasn't expecting you," she stuttered. "I . . . we . . . the students and I . . . we aren't prepared for an inspection." She chewed her lower lip. "If we'd known, we could have arranged some displays. Maybe even a program. But —"

"I didn't want any special preparation," Morgan said. "I just want to see your day-to-day operation. And don't fret about it, please. I'm only here to see how I can help you."

The teacher wasn't reassured. "Have there been any complaints?"

Morgan knew how she felt. Not so long ago she herself had dreaded visits from supervisors. Especially unscheduled visits.

"No, no complaints," she said. "And if it isn't convenient for me to come tomorrow —"

Arin shrugged. "Why not?" She managed a halfhearted smile. "You can go down with me in the morning and see the whole school day. Such as it is."

They agreed, and Arin left. "A standoffish sort," Elsie said. "No one knows her very well."

Morgan suspected that the young teacher was probably only shy. She knew from her files that this was Arin Molino's first assignment, and she remembered well the stresses and insecurities. Elsie, though, was cut from another cloth and wouldn't understand.

The party of skiers got up to leave, too. One of them came over to Morgan. "Borstrup says you'd like to go out on the snow for the late colors. We're all going. We have a sled and a driver, and you're welcome to join us.

"You, too," he added to Elsie.

"I hate the snows," Elsie said curtly. "I go out for only one reason, and there's not enough time at night to get there."

Morgan accepted with thanks. Karla provided her with an insulated parka, boots, and a pair of skis.

The groundsled took them away from the sea fogs to an area north of town and around the mountain. Argus hung glowing, surrounded by halos of gold and carmine and deep violet, at the edge of a sloping snow plain of shimmering beauty. There was no wind, and they skied with only light masks. Morgan had been warned about the illusion of warmth and resisted the temptation to remove hers. The air was sharply metallic, but it did not bother her at all. Her movements were dreamlike, her feet in a coruscating shower of sparks, her body bathed in a rainbow.

✳ 5 ✳

In the morning, Morgan tramped down the mountain road with Arin Molino. The temperature had fallen during the night, freezing the muddy slush into hard ridges. In the harbor below, new frazil ice lay on the surface of the water like an oily film, and farther off, on the open ocean, a huge chunk of pack ice gleamed orange and amber as Argus rose beyond it.

Both women were well bundled, but they battled a northern wind. Despite Morgan's ski mask, her lips were too stiff to move by the time they gained the shelter of the school.

It was one large room, its bare flooring boot-scarred, with a traditional chalkboard and desks in rows. It resembled a dozen classrooms Morgan had taught in.

She blew into her cupped hands to thaw her mouth. "These schools don't change much, do they, for all their exotic locations?" she said when she could speak again. She gave Arin what was meant to be a we're-in-this-together grin.

"I don't know. I suppose not," Arin said. She gazed around the room as if she were seeing it herself for the first time.

Morgan suspected what Arin must be thinking: I should have brightened it up. I should have tacked up art and samples of good work. I should have mopped the floor.

"It looks fine," Morgan said. Someone had been in to fire the stove, and when the two women removed their outer wraps, it was even tolerably warm.

The young teacher was dressed in a black sweater and pants, and her hair was tightly confined with combs and clips. There was no hiding her tension. "Nothing here is what I had expected," she said. "But I do the best I can." She moved stiffly to her desk and set out her lesson plans.

Morgan followed her and glanced at the open folder. "Nicely done," she said. "Exactly what I like to see. Everything organized. Everything prepared." She tried again with an encouraging smile.

Arin, however, would not respond. "I follow procedures," she said. "If you'll excuse me, I have to get the room ready." She avoided looking at Morgan as she bustled about, rearranging desks, laying out supplies, writing with quick strokes on the chalkboard.

The children began to arrive. Morgan lent a hand with the coats and boots, then sat back to watch.

The routine was familiar. Arin had divided the sixteen children into skill-related groups, and she divided her time among them. They ranged in age from six to twelve, about half of them with snowgrubber eyes and complexions. Morgan studied the roster and found names like Malmivaara, Maakala, Kylmasaari.

They regarded Morgan with shy, curious stares. The smallest child, a towheaded boy, saw Morgan watching him and burst into tears. Arin took the youngster on her lap. He mumbled something to her and she whispered back, wiping his nose and comforting him with a hug.

The teacher glanced uneasily at Morgan as she led the child back to his seat, then busied herself immediately with a reading group. Morgan began to move among the groups, too, helping where she could.

The children stared, then giggled. Arin spoke sharply and the gigglers froze, along with Morgan's hopes of establishing a rapport with them.

The children were well grounded in the basics, Morgan saw, and some were reading beyond grade level. Arin kept an orderly room, and there had been that telling show of compassion. The young teacher had no reason to be so uneasy, and Morgan longed for an opportunity to tell her so.

Arin taught a short half day to enable the students who lived farthest away to return home before the afternoon sleet storms. When the last child was gone, she tidied up the room and banked the stove. "I can make coffee," she said. "The local version. It's pretty bad, but I suppose you're used to it by now. Would you like a cup before we start back to the lodge?"

"Please." Now, perhaps, Arin would relax.

But the teacher was still on edge, clattering cups and spilling while she poured. When they were settled at two of the larger desks, she visibly braced herself. "So tell me, how did I do?"

Morgan smiled as reassuringly as she could. "I told you

before, I didn't come to make judgments. But don't worry, you're doing fine. As much like a pro as anyone I've seen."

Arin expelled a breath. She finally smiled back at Morgan.

"These primitive schools are difficult for anyone," Morgan continued. "And yet the Corps always sends them the newest probationers. How do you feel about the assignment?"

Arin hesitated a moment. "The truth, and you won't hold it against me?"

"Of course not! I wouldn't have asked unless I wanted an honest answer."

"You won't be surprised, then. I hate it! Not the children — I'm quite fond of them — but the place. I assumed when I got the posting to Jaspre that I'd be working in Friisland or the Grace Islands, not out here at the end of the world. I'll stick it out, for the rest of my term, but after that . . . I don't want to leave the Corps, but I couldn't take another year here."

"I understand how you feel, and it's a real problem. We need you here, with your experience this year. We've been criticized for rotating teachers too often."

"I mean it. I'm at the end of my rope!"

Morgan sighed. "I'll recommend that you get something better. You'll have paid your dues. Now, what can I do to make it easier for you?"

Arin refilled the coffee cups as they discussed programs and supplies and, finally, the students. "I was surprised at the makeup," Morgan said. "I thought they'd all be snowgrubbers. Where do the others come from?"

"Not all Lumislanders are grubbers," Arin explained. "We get visitors from the south, like Elsie, who stay on for one reason or another. Ski enthusiasts who find work in the canneries. Fishermen. If it weren't for their families, we'd hardly have a school at all, since most grubbers live out on the snows. It's only recently, I understand, that they've been sending their youngsters here in any numbers. There's been prejudice on both sides."

"These grubbers . . . they live out there alone?"

"Some, but mostly in settlements they call camps. Jarmo and Jarkko Kylmasaari come from a grubber camp up past Second Station Lodge. They're boarding in town with a relative for the school term."

"Have you ever had any children from Anders Ahlwen's camp? You know, the man Elsie hates so much?"

"He's got several camps, and yes, I had one girl, at the beginning of the term. I had to ask her to leave. She was too . . . disturbing."

"In what way?"

"She frightened the other children. They said she could see into their heads and put the 'bad sight' on them."

"An evil eye! Surely you didn't believe such nonsense."

"No, but the parents did. They threatened to pull their own children out, and you know, we're supposed to be responsive to their wishes."

Morgan nodded. "Yes. Teach only what we're asked, and to whom. Yet the little girl's parents wanted her to be educated, too."

Arin raised her chin and said, "But there were more of the others."

"I didn't mean to imply blame. You did the right thing. I wonder, though — couldn't you have tutored the child privately?"

The teacher fingered the handle of her cup. "I suppose I could have, but . . ." Her gaze shifted defensively. "Actually, I don't like to be around them, either. You see, it's not just Elsie. No one trusts Ahlwen or his followers. They're different; you can see it in their faces and in their eyes. There are stories about things they can do that aren't . . . natural."

"Like what?"

"Moving things — huge, heavy things — that no human could possibly manage. Seeing through walls. Hurting or healing, without lifting a finger."

Morgan felt a prickle along the surface of her skin. "Karla said something like that, about Ahlwen having the power. She said it came from the snow, and something about a journey."

Arin lowered her voice to barely above a whisper, though there was no one to overhear. "There's supposed to be a focal point, an axis, where the colors of Argus are brightest. To get there you have to go up into the glacier country, and you have to go alone. A sort of a proving. Everyone who makes the journey, if he lives, comes back changed. Either he has the power or he is mad."

Arin spoke as if she believed it. Karla, now, Morgan could understand. But Arin, who was educated . . . "Who would want to make such a trip?" Morgan asked.

"A surprising number of people, mostly grubbers. Most of them die. And of the ones who survive, most go out of their minds. Sometimes trekkers run into them, wandering the ice by day and howling at night from their burrows. They live like animals, dangerous ones, hunting anything that moves. You'd best go armed if you trek past Third Station Lodge. And never ski alone, even around here."

"This Ahlwen — he's the leader of these . . . seekers?"

"Apparently he's got their absolute loyalty."

"Have you ever seen him?"

She shuddered. "No, and I wouldn't want to. I don't even ski anymore, not since so many people have disappeared."

"Skiers? I went out last night, and no one in the group said anything about that."

"The lodge management keeps it quiet. It would ruin their business."

Morgan recalled her euphoria as she had glided across a frozen sunset. "I'm glad I didn't know." It would certainly have dampened her pleasure.

The room was rapidly chilling as the stove cooled. The storm came, pounding on the roof and rattling the windows. "I'm afraid we stayed too long," Arin said. "We'll be in for it, going home." She checked her watch. "Let's get outside. It's endshift at the cannery, and if we're lucky we can catch Elsie."

They bundled up and huddled on the porch. Icy sleet descended in torrents, and after a freezing quarter hour they flagged down the crawler.

Elsie motioned the two women to hop on, then pointed up the street and shouted. "A couple of stops, then I'll swing by the lodge for you two."

The bus was packed with oilskin-garbed men and women.

Strident voices competed with sonorhythm from half a dozen handsets, and the air was redolent with fish odors.

The noise abated as Morgan and Arin found seats. Morgan drew curious stares.

"My boss," Arin said to everyone in general. "Checking out the school."

Interrupted conversations resumed and Morgan listened to the comments around her: "Missing two days now." "What we ought to do is march on that camp and clear them all out." "You try it. You heard what happened to Pohjala when he went after his kid."

A burst of profanity was followed by, "They say he's got the crazies working for him up past Third Station. Can't no one get into his camp there."

The bus pulled up in front of the tavern and disgorged half the cannery workers. More got off at various side streets as they chugged up to the lodge.

Elsie swung open the bus door. "Don't forget," she reminded Morgan, "we'll be starting tomorrow at daybreak."

Uneasy from the talk she had just heard and from her discussion with Arin, Morgan was tempted to beg off. Elsie, however, was gone before she could open her mouth.

She would see her later, Morgan thought. She followed Arin inside, and after a late lunch she tried again to call Friishaven.

This time she reached both Jazmin and Arnie.

There was nothing pressing at the office, Jazmin reported. And there had been nothing more about Morgan in the newspapers.

Arnie announced that another job lead had fizzled. "Looks

85

like I'll be free to visit you," he said. "We're ready any time, all three of us. When shall we come?"

They made plans for the next week. "How are Matt and Dee?" Morgan asked.

"Matt's fine. Misses you, of course. He's out in back now, playing with a friend from school. Shall I call him?"

"No, just give him my love. And Dee — is she any better?"

"I think so. In fact, yes, I'm sure she is. We got her lab tests back, and they show nothing wrong at all. I got her the tutor, and she's settled down to study. Justin DiVoto's been giving her the rush — lunch and dinner every day."

"Is she eating? Let me talk to her if she's there."

Dee sounded guarded. Arnie wanted her to go back to the Academy, and she supposed she ought to try. No, she hadn't called the Zoological Institute. She didn't seem to have the time. Arnie and Justin . . . she was always so busy . . .

The phone crackled with static, and Dee's last words were lost. Morgan had heard enough, though, to tell that Arnie was wrong. Dee was still stressed, and no wonder, pushed and pulled in so many directions. At least she would keep her own hands off, Morgan vowed. No more about the Zoological Institute. She wished she could persuade Arnie as well, but she knew that wouldn't be so easy.

When Elsie came in, Morgan was so preoccupied about Dee that she didn't say anything to her after all about the trip to see Britt.

✳6✳

Outside the lodge in the early morning, the air was crackling cold and still. Morgan read fifteen degrees below the freezing mark on the porch thermogauge. It would be colder in the interior, she knew, and she had dressed accordingly, in borrowed fur-lined gear.

Argus was barely visible as a faint amber haze, and the real sun was obscured by low-lying dark clouds that promised the usual sleety coastal rain. Morgan was glad to be escaping it, though she was feeling apprehensive about the journey ahead.

Elsie had rented a small jetsled for the first stage of their travel. "It'll take us three hours to get to First Station in this," she said. "On skis, it's a day's trip. We can leave the sled at the station and trek from there to Ahlwen's camp. It's only an hour or so on skis and snowshoes."

"Can't we take the sled all the way?" In it, they would be well protected.

"No, the camp is up in the mountains, and it takes a grubber to handle a sled there. But don't worry, we'll be safe enough." Elsie opened her parka to reveal a stunner and a scattergun.

Morgan was not reassured. "What kind of trouble are you expecting?"

"None that I can't handle," Elsie said. Reading Morgan's face, she amended her words: "They're a bunch of weirdos up there, but they're no threat."

"What about those — whatever they are — they call 'crazies'? Yesterday, on the bus, people were talking scared."

"Is that what's bothering you? Naw, there are no crazies below Third Station. They're all out on the glaciers." She patted her midsection. "These babies are just a little extra security."

Morgan climbed into the sled. She had given her word, and it was too late for misgivings.

Elsie secured the canopy and eased into pulse power. They maneuvered slowly down the rutted street, through town and around the westernmost ridge of the mountains. Once on the snow plain, Elsie turned on the jets and the sled fairly flew, stirring up a wake that followed them like a white cloud.

With Argus still behind the peaks, the snow was a ghostly gray expanse that blended imperceptibly with the sky. They breakfasted on protein cubes and hot tea from Elsie's thermos, and an hour later the satellite was visible in the southwest. Gradually, fingers of purple and orange flame spread across the snow-covered tundra.

The plain extended ahead for limitless miles, an immensity of shimmering color that belied its true desolation. To the east rose the line of mountains, their contours softened and richly painted with a covering of Argus-lit snow. There was no sound but the soft whoosh of the jets, and no sign of human habitation. The only life they encountered was a single herd of humpbacked, shaggy-coated quadrupeds.

"Hirvisen," Elsie said. "They're foraging for buried lichen. Out here where it's exposed and windy, the snow's actually not too deep."

"Was that a grubber's herd?" Morgan asked.

Elsie shrugged. "Maybe. They're supposed to be living out here somewhere."

There was no trace of the snowgrubbers, however, or of any civilization, until they sighted the black outcroppings, jagged spires of rock erupting from the snow, that heralded First Station. The outpost consisted of a supply depot and store, a couple of sheds that housed the snow patrol equipment, a smaller version of the Lumisatama Lodge, and a scattering of ice igloos.

They had hot soup and bread at the lodge, in a dining room empty of guests except for the two of them. The proprietor, a wizened snowgrubber, did his best to try to talk them out of visiting Ahlwen's camp. "We don't have no truck with that bunch," he said. "Strange doin's there. Near ruined my business." He recognized Elsie. "You're the one been there before, lookin' for your friend."

"This time I'm bringing her out," Elsie said.

The man regarded her impassively. "You'll be the first."

They received even less encouragement at the snow patrol shed where they left their sled. "It'll be a useless trip," said the bearded young grubber on duty. "They run a tight camp. No one around here likes them much, but so far they've not crossed the law."

Which law, Morgan wondered, SEF or Jasprian? Technically, she knew, they should be the same, but the snowgrubbers had been here long before the Force. Morgan had the feeling that SEF would have cleaned out the troublesome camp without compunction, but the snow patrol was run by Lumislanders. She rather wished it were otherwise.

"You can't take anyone from a camp forcibly," the man warned.

"I know," Elsie said.

"Are you sure you don't want an escort?"

"No, I think we'll have better luck alone." Elsie checked Morgan's ski bindings and adjusted both of their packs. "All set?"

"You're certain you know the way?" Morgan asked. It was her last chance to back out. She opened her mouth to say more, but Elsie was already sliding across the packed, dirty snow of the compound.

"As well as the palm of my hand," she called back over her shoulder. "I could find it in my sleep."

The moment was gone. Morgan caught up with Elsie and kept pace. They left the buildings of the station behind as they headed east toward a horizon of broken ridges and peaks bathed in Argus fire. Around their feet, in the fresh snow, each crystalline flake glowed like a miniature gem.

A flurry blew across their faces, coating Morgan's goggles. "Is it likely to storm?" she asked with new concern.

"Not much chance," Elsie replied. "Not this far from the coast. We may get a light snowfall, but that's all."

Morgan relaxed. Elsie, after all, had made the trip safely many times. She began to enjoy the beauty and the exercise. The top layer of snow was dry and loose, above a frozen undercrust that provided a good skiing surface. Only Morgan's face was exposed to the cold, and it was heavily greased. The steady rhythm of her arms and legs and the ever-changing colors had an almost hypnotic effect. Elsie had to grab Morgan's arm to get her attention.

They stopped while Elsie took a compass reading. She altered their course, and the surface of the plain began to dip and rise as they entered an area of foothills. Soon they were skirting ice cliffs and canyons where they moved from sunlit brilliance to dark shadows. When they could no longer proceed on skis, they exchanged them for snowshoes, strapping the skis and poles to their pack frames.

Elsie stopped frequently for bearings, nodded, and forged ahead. They followed a gully that ran to a dark hole in one of the mountain walls, which proved to be the maw of an enormous ice cave.

Morgan stood still in her tracks as figures dressed in shaggy hirvisen fur appeared from all sides, surrounding them.

"Let us through," Elsie demanded. "We want to get inside. We've come to see Britt Halsemer."

"If you'll give us your weapons," the nearest of the guards said. He reached out to Elsie.

"We have none." Elsie showed her empty hands.

"The two. The stunner and the scattergun." The guards moved closer. They were unarmed, but their bearing spoke clearly that they were to be obeyed. Their faces, what Morgan could see of them beneath the shadowy hoods, were snowburned to near black.

Morgan felt their combined scrutiny as almost a physical force. She looked up into slitted eyes that changed color like the snow. "You can come in," said the one who seemed to be the leader. He nodded at Morgan.

"What about me?" Elsie had handed over her guns and stood with legs apart and hands on her hips, glaring. "Do I have to wait out here and freeze while you jokers make up your minds?"

The guards conferred. "Come on, then," the spokesman said. "Follow me, both of you."

He led the way into an ice-walled room some ten meters square, with archways that opened to interior spaces. Skis and snowshoes and an assortment of bone and metal implements unfamiliar to Morgan ranged along one wall, and along the other stood handsleds and a single larger, jet-powered one.

Morgan and Elsie removed their snowshoes, skis, and packs. "You can wait in there," the man said to Elsie, directing her to the opening nearest the main entrance.

"Hold on." Elsie grabbed his arm. "When will I get to see Britt?"

"You can't. She's given orders: she doesn't wish it."

Elsie started to protest, but he silenced her with a look. "You can give your messages to this one." He indicated Morgan. "She can come with me."

Elsie cursed, sputtering in anger. When the man ignored her, she turned desperately to Morgan. "They'll try to trick you," she warned. Her words spilled out, frantic and urgent.

"Be sure it's Britt you talk to. She's a tall woman, taller than me, but thin. She's got strawberry blond hair that's turning gray, and she wears it in a braid. Gray-green eyes and a black mole on her right cheek. Be sure it's her. Tell her I've been here five times now. Find out why she can't leave. Tell her I'm waiting and she can leave with us." She took a breath. "It's up to you now. I'm depending on you." Her voice broke. "Tell her I love her."

Morgan assented to everything. A figure in a quilted coverall appeared from one of the inner rooms, beckoned, and she followed.

They passed through a labyrinth of passages, ice tunnels bored precision-straight, their smooth walls glistening under glow-globes, branching one way and then another until Morgan lost all sense of direction. She caught glimpses, through curtained doorways, of softly lit cave rooms filled with activity and others with single occupants. Her guide stopped before one such small chamber and indicated to Morgan that she should enter.

The tall woman who rose to welcome Morgan matched Elsie's description of Britt. She was dressed in a loose jacket and pants of soft hide, with nothing on her feet but thin-looking moccasins.

Morgan had no desire to remove even her parka. The air was less bitter than outdoors, but she felt no thawing in her numb cheeks.

Aside from the temperature, however, the room looked surprisingly comfortable. The ice walls were partially covered with the woven hangings that seemed to be favored by Lumislanders, and the floor was carpeted with soft, living moss. There were no furnishings except for a low table made of stretched hide and a fur-covered couch, littered with sketch papers and a pad, where Britt had been working.

"You came with Elsie? It's a long trek from Satama; I hope you didn't make it just because of me." Her voice was low and pleasant. "Please, sit down," she invited. "Take off your wraps; you must be stifling." A corner of her mouth curved up.

She knows very well how cold I am, Morgan thought. She hugged her arms as she sank into the soft furs. "Of course we came because of you. You must know how worried Elsie is."

"She shouldn't be."

"Will you come with me and talk to her?"

"No, I don't want to see her."

"Are you afraid?" Perhaps Elsie was right about coercion. Morgan grew bolder. "Is it because seeing Elsie might break whatever spell is keeping you here?"

Britt showed no offense. "No, there's no danger of that. But it *will* make it more difficult for me, and I have so much yet to learn. I can't afford to dissipate my energies on a useless emotional confrontation."

"Then you do still have feelings for Elsie. Her feelings for you haven't changed at all, you know."

Britt sighed. "I'm sorry for her, but she has to learn to let go. Yes, I still care for her, but I know her, and she'd only try to drag me away from what I've found here. And I can't let her do that. Not when I have the possibility of breaking through physical barriers. Of growing within myself." A rapt expression illuminated her face. "Of touching the power."

94

Chemicals, Morgan thought. Yet Britt exhibited no physical symptoms.

"No, I'm clean," Britt said with startling clairvoyance. "There are no drugs in this camp. Whatever you see, whatever these people can do, it's all natural."

Morgan withheld opinion. "Tell me about when you first came here," she said. "What happened to make you want to stay."

Britt sat with clasped hands. "I felt the power in the snow from the first day we left Satama. Strange, isn't it? To Elsie, it was just pretty colors. But I'd never felt so well, so *alive*. Then I sprained my ankle and we were taken here. I knew immediately it was a place like no other. What did you think when you saw the tunnels, all of this?" She gestured around the room. "*He* did it, you know. He made this camp when he came back from his first journey, full of the power. With nothing but his hands, they say."

And a little help from a laser drill, Morgan thought. But she nodded to Britt to continue.

"An old man healed my ankle with a touch, and I asked to meet some more of the people who lived here. They took me to Anders Ahlwen, and I talked to him. No one tried to keep me here; I begged to be allowed to stay." Her face glowed, as it had before. "I've come so far, everyone says. My work, look at it." She gathered up her sketches and handed them to Morgan. "I could never have done that before."

Lifelike faces in black and white stared up at Morgan. Vivid snow scenes in chalk. Abstract swirls of color that leaped from the paper.

95

"That last one, it's Argus power as I imagine it. As I'll see it when I make the journey."

Morgan stared in disbelief. "I've heard of it, of how dangerous it is. Surely you wouldn't take the chance."

"It's why I'm here, preparing myself. When I'm ready, I'll go."

"But why?"

Another voice answered from the doorway. "Britt is one of those who have been touched by the power and cannot rest until they experience it fully."

The curtain opened to admit a short, slender man. In appearance he was not distinguished: grubber eyes, a smooth but snow-darkened face, and close-clipped black hair that grew low on his brow. Like the pelt of a puerhu, Morgan thought, remembering pictures she had seen of the seal-like creatures of Jaspre's northern oceans.

It was hard to estimate his age, but Morgan guessed forty or so. He was dressed in a faded denim coverall, with sandals on his bare feet. His speech revealed him as off-planet educated, an anomaly among the grubbers she had met.

Britt spread her hands in a gesture of welcome. "Teacher," she murmured.

Morgan guessed immediately who it was.

"*Rauha,*" Anders Ahlwen said. "Peace." He included Morgan in his smile.

"If you wish to speak to our visitor in private . . ." Britt made as if to leave.

"No, stay if you wish," Ahlwen said. He sank cross-legged upon the moss, facing Morgan. "Everyone here hopes to make the journey," he said. "Some have already done so. Not all

96

are strong enough, however, and I try to discourage those who I feel have little chance of success."

"And you think Britt does? A Friishaven city woman who has always lived in comfort? Alone in a glacial wilderness where you can't even measure the cold?"

"Britt has more resources than you imagine. She has already learned to control her metabolism and her body temperature."

In response, Morgan pulled her parka more closely about her. "Don't you people believe in fires?"

His mouth twitched. "Yes, most of us have oil stoves in our rooms. Britt, being a new disciple, has embraced our discipline perhaps more rigorously than is strictly necessary."

A flush appeared on Britt's cheeks. "If I'm to make the journey —"

Ahlwen held up his hand. "*Rauha*. You will do it."

The flush subsided. "Shall I get an oilring?" she asked.

"Not on my account," Morgan said. Then she turned to Ahlwen. "I'll be leaving right now if Britt is determined to stay. I only wanted to see if she was being held under duress." She made a motion to rise but did not complete it. "This power," she said. "This journey. What is it, really? I know you'll say it comes from the snow. I've heard that before, but surely it can't be true."

"In a way, it is." His voice was soft, but with an underlying intensity. "The power is a form of solar energy. The snow is a transforming agent — the second one. The first is Argus."

"Transforming? You mean when the solar rays are reflected back to Jaspre?"

"Yes. The Argus engineers wrought more than they ever realized. The snows merely complete the job, focusing the energy to us in a form we can use if we allow it to enter us.

"For that, we make the journey. Oh, you can receive some benefits from the snow, even down at Satama. The old-time grubbers all felt it. They've always had healers and soothsayers. Witch women with second sight. There was one in a camp near the one where I grew up, and she told me about a place in the far north where all the colors come together. She had been there, she said, though not many believed her.

"I did, though. I'd spent most of my waking hours on the snow, and I knew what it could do. I promised myself that someday I'd find the place, but it wasn't until I came back from Centauri Astra — yes, I studied with the mystics there on a SEF scholarship that was intended for other purposes — that I accomplished my goal."

"You found this . . . place?"

"I found mine." He shifted his gaze to Britt, who sat rapt, hugging her knees. "I suspect that for each person it is a different spot."

Morgan frowned. "You're saying, then, that it's an inner journey?"

"Partly. Oh, the trek is real enough." He held out his gnarled hands, which were scarred and discolored, the fingertips missing. "I stayed too long, with too little care for myself. I was overwhelmed.

"I didn't recruit my followers. Like Britt, they simply came. As I said, there are many who have tasted the power and want to receive more of it."

Something about his words made Morgan uneasy. "And when there are enough of you, what do you propose to do with this power?"

"Not what you are thinking. Nothing political that would threaten SEF or the grubbers who choose not to join us. I have a vision for Lumisland, the way I would like to see it someday. A place where Argus-adepts could live freely, without interference, to explore the full psychic potentials of the human race.

"That is all in the future, though. Right now I am working with Britt and a half dozen others to help them achieve the necessary state of heightened awareness. The journey, to them, will pose no life-threatening dangers."

Morgan shook her head. "I still don't believe it. I think it's insane for Britt to go."

"Someday you may understand," Ahlwen said.

"I don't think so." A glance at her watch revealed to Morgan that she had stayed far too long. "Elsie will be worried. Britt, will you show me the way out?"

Ahlwen rose, too. "I will. Perhaps I can convince this formidable Elsie to stop making her useless trips."

"Yes, do," Britt urged. "She'll see that she needn't be afraid for me."

"Shall I give her a message?" Morgan asked.

"Only that I'm happy," Britt said.

Ahlwen guided Morgan back through the tunnels. Again, she caught glimpses of crowded rooms. "I thought you said you had only a half dozen disciples," she observed. "I've seen at least ten times that many."

"I said I was *training* half a dozen. Most of these you see

99

are already adepts. Others are living here for reasons of their own, probably because they enjoy the lifestyle."

"You mean, to be near you."

"That, or my gardens." They paused before a room where brilliant Argus light shone through a clear roof. A hanging arrangement of ice slabs focused the light directly on leafy masses of green plants growing densely in long vats.

Morgan would have asked for a closer look except for troubled thoughts about an impatient Elsie. "Is this a typical grubber camp?" she asked as they hurried on.

"Far from it. Most of them are extremely primitive. A scattering of igloos. In the mountains, a communal ice cave. I wish more of my people could live this way. Perhaps someday it will come about."

"Unless Argus Two goes up." Morgan thought fleetingly of Nurmi's prohibition against discussing the proposed new satellite, but she was too far away from Friishaven to be deterred. "Have you heard of it? What would happen then?"

His dark face stiffened. "Yes, I've heard. In that case, we would lose everything."

"You don't think the effects could be duplicated?"

"No. There are no colors in the southern snow zone. Another Argus would destroy more than your misguided SEF could ever hope to gain."

They were back at the entry room. Elsie was waiting on a bench in a small alcove, watched by one of the grubber guards.

She sprang to her feet. "Where's Britt? Didn't you get to see her? God, you've been gone for hours." She caught sight of Ahlwen. "Who's this?"

"Yes, I saw Britt, and she's fine. She wants to stay here, though."

Elsie started to protest. "I'll tell you about it on the way back," Morgan said. "This is Anders Ahlwen. I tried to get Britt to come talk to you, but she wouldn't. He came instead."

A roar erupted from Elsie's throat. She made a dash for the guard, pushed him against the wall, and seized her scattergun from his loosened grasp.

She raised it and aimed it at Ahlwen.

Morgan screamed. Anders Ahlwen stood taut as a stretched wire. A tremor shook his frame, and his narrowed eyes burned with a light that made Morgan turn away.

Elsie gave a single cry and slumped to the ground.

Ahlwen nodded to the guard. "Load her on a sled, and take them to First Station." He addressed Morgan. "She'll be all right. She's just stunned." He turned and walked off, back into the interior tunnel.

Elsie did not regain consciousness until they were nearly at the station. The sled-puller was uncommunicative, and Morgan was left to her own thoughts as she skied behind.

Ahlwen: what was he? Whatever he had done to Elsie was real enough, yet he was only human.

Argus power: was it a true phenomenon? She couldn't bring herself to believe in it either, despite everything she had seen and heard.

All around Morgan the snow pulsed with shimmering color. Britt said that she had never felt so alive. Morgan felt extraordinarily well, too, for all her strenuous journey. Had she been "touched," too, she wondered?

Healers. Visions. Heightened awareness. Was it more than pseudopsychic babble? Ahlwen had studied on Astra, where mystic cults proliferated. Undoubtedly he saw himself as some kind of prophet, even though he denied it.

Yet Britt had seemed truly happy. If she were conned, it was because of a need Ahlwen had met. Perhaps the camp *was* a paradise for some, Morgan thought. For those who needed the kind of anchor he provided.

Elsie called out, and Morgan skied abreast of the sled.

"Did I kill him?"

"No, he knocked you out." Morgan didn't say how.

Elsie appeared relieved. She recovered gradually and completely from her paralysis, but she was subdued for the remainder of the trek. Back in their sled, headed for Satama, neither woman had much to say.

✻7✻

Back in the Lumisatama Lodge, Morgan buried herself in make-work, anything to keep from thinking about what she had just experienced. She occupied a full day writing up requisitions for Arin's school, and another drafting long, encouraging letters to every East Region teacher. When a packet from Jazmin arrived, she seized it gratefully; more hours to fill practicing her signature and making minute corrections to unimportant documents.

Whatever savored of the familiar, she embraced. The lodge, without her family, was unbearably lonely. What if she were stuck here all year? Would Arnie and Dee and Matt move here, too?

It didn't seem likely, not with Satama such a dismal hole. There was the snow, of course, but even that was now suspect. Morgan waxed hot and cold, one moment wanting them all with her, the other thinking they would be better off in Friishaven.

The visit would be the deciding factor. Morgan made sure that their rooms were ready. Magnus brought in a double bed for her and Arnie, and set up two small rooms across the hall for Dee and Matt. She arranged for a ski trek with guides to First and Second Stations.

There would be no forays off the tourist paths. Surely, she told herself finally, they could all enjoy the beauty of the snows without any nonsense about its arcane powers.

The days passed with frustrating slowness, but finally Morgan was waiting in Elsie's bus at the wind-scoured airstrip. The plane unloaded a dozen strangers before she spotted three familiar figures, and only then, in her rush of relief, did she realize how much she had been afraid that they would not come.

"Over here! Over here!" She waved from the door of the bus while Elsie leaned on the horn.

Matt sprinted ahead and greeted her with a hug. "Mom! We saw the colored icebergs and some of the snow! I can't wait. When can we go out on it? Brrr, is it always this cold?"

Morgan pulled him inside and away from the door. Dee and Arnie arrived close behind him, Dee shivering as she sheltered under Arnie's cloak.

Morgan started to scold them, then remembered that she had arrived just as ill prepared. "Get in, get in," she urged.

Arnie's lips were cold and stiff when they kissed. "What about our bags?" he asked.

"I'll pick them up, soon as they're unloaded," Elsie said.

Morgan made introductions.

"I hope you'll enjoy your stay here in our little resort,"

104

Elsie said with a wry twist of her mouth. Morgan had warned her against making disparaging comments about Satama, and she contented herself with a single "Such as it is."

They took seats, and Elsie turned up the heat. "It's better than waiting in there," Morgan said, indicating the drafty terminal.

Arnie squeezed her hand. "I've missed you."

Morgan gazed at the three faces, reassuring herself. It was real; she was no longer alone.

"Jazmin sends a big hello," Arnie said. "And more paperwork."

"When did you see her?"

"Matt and I had dinner with her last night."

"Has she heard anything at all about when I might be able to go back?"

"No, that's particularly what I wanted to find out. But apparently Commander Nurmi's still playing it close. There've been more and more demonstrations against Argus Two and SEF, and needless to say he's not happy about it. Jazmin doesn't think there's much chance of his recalling you for a good while yet."

"So I'm still the sacrificial lamb."

"What does that mean, Mom?" Matt leaned over from the seat ahead.

"Are you always listening?" Morgan reached to tweak his cowlick, but he moved his head and escaped. "It means that the commander is trying to appease his critics by removing one of their minor irritants, which happens to be me. The term comes from — oh, I'll explain later, when we get settled."

Matt nodded. His attention was already on the mountains and the sea, his head swiveling from the windows on one side to those on the other. Dee sat beside him, huddled under a blanket Elsie had provided, not even glancing outside.

"She didn't feel well on the plane," Arnie said. "I don't know . . . I hope this trip isn't too much for her. Justin was very much against it."

"I can imagine." To Morgan, Dee didn't look any better. Her eyes had the same haunted quality, and her face was even more drawn. "Did you want to come?" Morgan asked her.

Dee turned to face them. "Oh, yes. Friishaven was getting so hectic, with all the marches. Some demonstration or other almost every day. I didn't want to go downtown anymore, not even with Justin. That's why I stopped the therapy." She looked up at Morgan anxiously. "Justin and Daddy said it was all right."

'Well, I'm glad you're here." Anything else could wait.

The other passengers were largely silent as they drove through the gray countryside. They passed the gravel pits and the furze-drying sheds, and Elsie gave short explanations. At the equipment garage in town she let off one group, who were going by sled directly to First Station Lodge.

"Is Anders Ahlwen still at his camp up there?" one of them asked.

Elsie nodded. "Unfortunately."

Morgan expected a tirade, but Elsie said no more. She had not mentioned Ahlwen or Britt since their return from his camp, and Morgan hoped she had given up her crusade.

Only Elsie's tightened mouth revealed her feelings. That

and the sharpness of her turns as she gunned the bus up the steep track.

"That was some driving!" Matt grinned as he hopped off, directly into the lake of slush that fronted the lodge.

Dee picked her way to a solid spot and looked around with a disappointed expression. "Don't make any judgments yet," Morgan begged. "It's completely different on the plain on the other side of the mountains. The sky is clear and there's nothing but colored snow, as far as you can see."

Arnie picked Dee up as if she were a child. "I'll carry you in," he said. "Those thin boots are no good here."

Morgan and Matt struggled with the luggage until Arnie returned to help. "Don't look so worried," he said. "We're not going to turn around and go back."

"You'll see," Morgan repeated. "It's better on the —"

Arnie interrupted her. "I know. I believe you. But what we came for is right here." They were inside the lodge, and he dumped the bags to give her a gentle shake and another kiss.

While the other guests registered, Morgan took her family upstairs. She had bribed Magnus Borstrup to provide more heat, and the rooms had lost their chilly edge. Arnie and Dee unpacked, while Matt emptied his duffel on the floor and declared himself ready for skiing.

"After dinner," Morgan promised. "We'll get in three or four hours then. Tomorrow, too. We all have to get in shape for the long trek."

Matt objected to resting, even when Morgan explained that they would be up late. Arnie threatened leaving him behind if he so much as yawned during dinner, and he reluctantly agreed to lie down for half an hour. When Morgan looked in on him ten minutes later, he was fast asleep.

Dee chose to nap, too. "I love the room," she said. Morgan had worried that it was too austere. "And the seclusion." Her window looked out upon rocks and black water.

Alone with Arnie, Morgan voiced her concerns about Dee, about whether she would have the stamina for a long stint of skiing. "We could all go for a ride in the sled instead," she said, "though it wouldn't be the same."

"Dee's stronger than she looks," Arnie said. "Give her a chance."

Morgan reserved judgment. "We'll see how it goes."

In this instance, Arnie's prediction proved correct. Magnus Borstrup and Karla took all of the lodge guests out on the plain for the twilight skiing, and Dee had no problem. Magnus led the group in a great circle that started on the gentle downhill slopes of the mountain foothills and ended with a two-hour stretch of flat trekking.

Matt and Dee were the only novices, but under Karla's instruction both of them caught on quickly. The three young people brought up the rear of the procession, with Arnie and Morgan in front of them. Morgan looked back frequently at first, but less often as she saw that they had no difficulty keeping pace.

Magnus Borstrup swooped back to check, too, then skied alongside Morgan. "They're naturals," he said. "Like born snowgrubbers. Another day's practice and you can set out for First Station."

"Will you go with us?" Arnie asked.

"I can't leave the lodge," Magnus said. "But my brother Vulpius has promised to go as guide. Him and Karla. They'll look after you fine."

Magnus returned to his lead position. The procession snaked through cold radiance as Argus in its slow setting illuminated the plain with wave after wave of pulsing color. Underfoot were the shattered crystalline gems, and in the distance, where the surface dipped, lakes of fire and molten gold.

Dee left her companions and shot off ahead and at a tangent to the line, moving with an easy, smooth rhythm. Remembering her own first time on the snow, Morgan knew how she felt: so entranced by her surroundings that the physical effort of skiing was nothing, her body inexhaustibly strong yet feather-light, seeming to melt into the glow around her.

Dee was in no danger — on the flat plain, everyone was plainly in sight — but Arnie moved off after her. Matt followed them, and Morgan dropped back to ski beside Karla.

The girl hastily replaced the dark goggles that had been dangling at her neck.

"Should you go without them like that?" Morgan asked. "I thought your eyes could get badly burned."

"Yes. I mean no, you shouldn't," Karla said, stammering. "Don't tell Dad. It was only for a few minutes."

"But why?"

"The feeling. It's so much more than what you get with the goggles. You feel like you could do anything. It's the Argus power."

Up ahead, the two inexperienced skiers flew like seasoned

veterans. There was something, certainly . . . Morgan pondered, then turned to Karla. "You said you'd heard Anders Ahlwen give a talk once. What did he say?"

"It was about what he'd learned on Astra. Psychic healing and how you could see into your body. Foretelling and things like that. He said how lucky we were to be living here in Lumisland, because with the snow, we could do much more even than the Astrans. Some of us more than others, but he said that he thought all of us grubbers had been affected, changed in some way by living on the snows."

"What kind of a reaction did he get?"

"Well, not very good. The tourists wanted him to do some tricks, and when he wouldn't, they laughed at him. The grubbers that were there, me and some of my friends, wanted to talk to him some more, but he said for us to come see him when we were older. I will, too. As soon as I'm eighteen. Dad can't stop me then."

Morgan looked ahead again, where Dee and Matt and Arnie were returning to the line. Suddenly she had a disturbing thought, almost a foreboding. "Have you talked to Dee about any of this?" she asked.

"No. Should I?"

"Do me a favor, please, and don't. Not a word."

"If you'll not tell Dad what I've been blabbing."

Morgan agreed to the deal, but she still felt uneasy. She didn't know how much she could trust Karla. She certainly couldn't keep her away from Dee, and the more she thought about it, the more she wished that Karla weren't coming with them on the trek.

There was nothing she could do about it now, though,

without appearing irrational. Which she told herself she probably was, reaching so far for new worries. Dee wasn't one to cultivate a sudden new friendship, and she and Karla would seem to have little in common.

Or so Morgan hoped.

Matt and Dee skied up to her.

"Did you see me, Mom, when I made that turn?" Matt's voice shrilled with excitement, and Morgan could imagine the rapt expression behind the goggles and mask.

"Terrific," she said. "But no more wandering off. Stay with the rest of us."

She said it more for Dee's benefit than Matt's. Dee nodded.

"Tired?" Morgan asked.

"No, I could go on forever," Dee said. "It's glorious."

The next day, the rapture was replaced by stiff joints and sore muscles. Magnus prescribed hot baths and massages for all of them, and another three-hour session on the snows.

They went out in the early afternoon rather than evening, to get plenty of rest for a dawn start for First Station. After the skiing, Morgan took care of Dee's rubdown while Arnie saw to Matt.

Dee purred under Morgan's hands. "Mmmm. More of that, please. I'll owe you forever."

"Just gain some weight and I'll be satisfied." The ridges of Dee's spine stood out much too sharply.

"I try," Dee said. "Really I do, but I just can't make myself eat enough. Maybe here I can do it. I feel so much better already."

"You said that about Friishaven, too, when you first came. Remember? What happened?"

Dee buried her face in the pillow. "Daddy . . . and Justin . . ." she mumbled.

Morgan lifted the girl's head. "I can't hear you."

Dee propped herself on an elbow. "I thought it would be different, being with all of you again. I thought it would be like home, like New Terra. But it isn't. In fact, in some ways it's almost like it was at the Academy."

"What do you mean?"

"The pressures. Dad thinks I should go back there, back to Earth, and he's got me studying that awful physics. I don't want to disappoint him again, but I just can't . . ." Her voice faded to a whisper.

"And Justin?"

She traced circles with her finger on the bed sheet. "I know what he wants. He's got my life all planned, too. He'd like me to be a sweet little SEF wife, making homes wherever he's sent. Giving parties for commanders and generals. Basking in his glory."

"Has he asked you?"

"No, but it's pretty obvious. He's given enough hints."

"You don't think much of that kind of a future, I gather."

"You're right."

"But do you love him?"

She sighed. "I don't know. It's been too fast. He's attractive, sure. I can tell how envious other women are. And he makes me feel . . . protected. But I don't think he really knows me at all. He's got this image of me as some sort of a delicate rare flower, and maybe I seem like that now, but it's just because I've not been well." She looked up at Morgan, entreating. "You know how strong I used to be. That harvester I ran. All those school prizes. That's how I want to be again, but not for the Academy or for Justin."

"For yourself," Morgan said. "I understand. And you'll do it. Look how well you've been doing skiing."

"I do feel better out there," Dee said. "And did you see me at lunch?"

"I noticed."

Dee beamed, so pleased with her improvement that Morgan buried her misgivings about the probable cause, just as she buried her guilt about once more falling into the same trap as Arnie and Justin, in trying to shield Dee from Karla's influence.

She didn't say anything to Arnie about Karla or Ahlwen. He was so elated when Dee ate a full dinner that Morgan hated to unload worries on him.

Later, when Elsie joined them for after-dinner coffee, Morgan was sorry she hadn't spoken to Arnie. "Could I go with you tomorrow?" the big woman asked. "I have to get to First Station right away, and the sleds are all taken."

"Why not?" Arnie said. "We plan to make it in a day, but that should be no problem for you. I imagine you're more fit than any of us."

"Why the urgency?" Morgan asked.

She could have bitten her tongue. Elsie lifted her chin, her face an angry color. "That rotten creep Ahlwen! Now he's got his hooks into Britt's money, and I'll be damned if I'll stand by while he bleeds her. I'm going to see him again, both of them, and have it out. She can play the fool if she likes, but she's not taking me down to ruin with her." She reached into her pocket and displayed a sheaf of printed forms. "These came in today's mail packet." She pushed two sheets across the table. "Here. She's withdrawn half of our joint account in the Friishaven bank. And this is a notice that she's put some land we own up for sale. They want my signature." She slapped down a third document. "Our flitter."

"What do you suppose she wants the money for?" Morgan said. "From what I saw in that camp, they live very simply."

Elsie snorted. "They say he's got a palace, back where he used to live, on Astra. They say he's got his own starship."

Matt and Dee were both wide-eyed. Arnie looked from Elsie to Morgan. "Won't one of you tell me what this is all about?"

Morgan nodded at Elsie. "Go ahead." It would be better for Dee to hear Elsie's version than Karla's.

Elsie spared no words painting a black picture of Ahlwen. She concluded: "And no one, not even SEF, will believe what a menace he is."

"How many followers would you say he has?" Arnie asked.

"No one knows. Maybe hundreds. He's got at least three camps. One not far from First Station, one around Third, and one on the glacier which no one but his people has ever seen."

Arnie turned to Morgan. "First Station? Why didn't you say anything about this? Especially since we'll be stopping so near."

Morgan tried to think of how to extricate herself. "Actually it's not so near," she protested. "The camp is off into the mountains." She drew a breath. "I didn't mention it because I didn't think you'd be interested. I didn't think you'd want to make a special trip to visit it."

"You thought right." Arnie patted Morgan's hand, and she relaxed.

"I've run into characters like that before," Arnie continued. "Swamis and messiahs and practitioners of you-name-it. It's too bad about your friend, Elsie. You'll be doing her a big favor if you refuse to sign any of those releases. When she comes to her senses, as most of those cult-followers do sooner or later, she'll thank you."

Elsie nodded vigorously and started in again on Ahlwen. Morgan looked away from her to the kitchen doorway, where Karla Borstrup rolled her eyes and waggled her fingers in a rude imitation of the older woman's harangue.

Dee, Morgan saw, was watching the display with frank curiosity.

Morgan frowned. It was hopeless, she thought. May as well try to stop the tide as restrain Karla. Still, Morgan continued to do what she could, hushing Elsie and getting everyone into the sitting room for a round of card games. Karla would be busy washing dishes, and Dee would be out of her reach at least for that evening.

✳8✳

Vulpius Borstrup was a squint-eyed, heavy-bearded bear of a figure dressed in skins and shaggy furs. He met Morgan and her party at the beginning of the snow plain, having skied in from a mountain camp.

His response to the introductions was a single grunt. He studied Dee, frowned deeply, and muttered to Karla.

"He says Dee is too skinny and she'll freeze in those clothes," Karla said.

Dee was wearing the same insulated gear Morgan had bought in Satama for all of them. It had been fine on the other two occasions they had been out, but now, with Argus still behind the mountain, the cold was a biting, pressing heaviness in the sunless sky. Dee swung her arms and stamped around in small circles, and Morgan could see that she felt it more than the others.

"We'll be okay once we get moving," Arnie said. "And we'll have Argus light in — what? — two hours?"

"About that," Morgan said. "But . . . I don't know —"

Karla had been conferring with Vulpius. "Uncle says he'll take care of Dee. We know a grubber camp nearby, and he can get something better for her to wear. He says let's go."

They moved off, seven figures in a ragged line. They turned toward the mountains, and before long Morgan found herself laboring. There was none of the exhilaration of the other times, nothing but hard pushing and lungs that strained and cold that cut through her mask. She longed for the relief that Argus would bring, especially for Dee, who straggled near the end of the line.

Fortunately, they did not have far to go. Vulpius halted at the top of a hill, where a smooth white valley lay cupped between it and the next rise. House-sized snow mounds grew out of the ridge at the far end, the protected, leeward side, and Morgan could see tiny figures moving between them.

In an instant the figures were gone. Vulpius motioned for Dee and Morgan to go with him, and the others to wait with Karla.

They skied down quickly and easily.

Vulpius uttered a long, low whistle as they approached the camp, and a fur-clothed man emerged from one of the mounds.

"Wait here," Vulpius said. He went forward to speak with the man, and Morgan and Dee looked the camp over curiously.

They had apparently interrupted a butchering operation. A partially cut carcass lay in chunks upon the snow, and stretched tight between pegs was a drying puerhu hide.

Three women came out of the entrance tunnel of another mound, smiled shyly at Morgan and Dee, and resumed their work. Their faces were uncovered and very brown, their eyes all but hidden by the overhanging lids. They used hand-sized knives to cut up the carcass into small bits, expertly stripping off fat and setting it aside, removing sinews and flipper fibers and selected bones.

"Come on," Vulpius said, beckoning. He led the way to one of the round snowhouses. "Woman in there has a hir-visen parka and boot liners. Ought to fit the little gal. Go on in," he urged. "*Jo,* both of you."

Morgan stooped as she entered an upward-sloping tunnel. The room inside had a translucent window and a ventilation grate in the ceiling. The walls and floor were covered with hides, and it was reasonably warm. Later in the day it would be almost cozy, Morgan thought; with the window facing south and west, there would be Argus light shining in.

A woman held out a brown fur garment. "Vulpius says you need."

"It's so light," Dee marveled. She passed the fur to Morgan. "Feel."

"Put it on quickly," Morgan said. "The others are waiting for us, probably freezing."

Dee removed her store-bought parka and slipped into the grubber one. It came to just above her knees, but it was cut to allow easy movement. The ruff was of a snowy white fur, as soft as down.

"And these, in the boots," the woman said. "From a calf, warm for the feet."

Dressed in her new gear, Dee pirouetted with delight.

"What can we give you?" Morgan asked.

"Oh, for Vulpius . . . it's all right." The woman shrugged.

"No, please," Morgan insisted. She offered Dee's old parka. "Can you use this?"

The woman laughed. "No. No good."

"You takin' too long!" came a bellow from outside.

"Then thank you, and we'll settle with Vulpius," Morgan said. Dee echoed the thanks, and they left.

Vulpius hustled them out of the camp. "What do we owe for the clothes?" Morgan asked. "The woman wouldn't say."

"You like, eh?" Vulpius grinned at Dee.

"The furs are beautiful," Dee said. "And I'm so much warmer I can hardly believe it."

The guide turned to Morgan. "Them're not to keep. Just a loan. Too much work in 'em to give away or sell."

"Oh, I hope I didn't insult her, then," Morgan said.

Vulpius shrugged.

As they labored up the slope, Morgan fought embarrassment. But Dee moved with ease in her new furs, and Morgan told herself that that was all that should concern her.

They found Arnie and Elsie stamping around on the top of the hill while Karla and Matt practiced turns. "Let's go," Vulpius said.

They headed west to meet the rays of the satellite as it appeared from behind the mountains. By midmorning, the world around them was transformed.

Argus still wore the colors of daybreak. This far north, it was always low in the southern horizon and long in its rising and setting. It created no seasons, nor did the real sun. With Jaspre's circular orbit and only slight axial tilt, there were no great differences of day length, as in the northern latitudes of Earth. There were no summer thaws or winter freezes, only the blanketed tundra; and farther north, the great glacial ice cap, a vast palette for the splashings of Argus.

And Argus's rays began to have their energizing effect on Morgan, as strength flowed into her body. The line picked up speed.

Arnie skied up to Morgan. "Dee's doing fine," he said. "And I can't keep up with Matt."

The boy was in the lead with Vulpius. Dee skied with Karla, off to one side, deep in conversation.

Morgan wondered if Karla even remembered her promise. She was sixteen years old, Morgan had learned from Magnus, and probably as passionate in her opinions as anyone that age.

Danny at sixteen had thought he knew more than his father about everything concerning the farm. Morgan still winced at the memory of their quarrels. Dee, however, had been different. If she had ever had rebellious thoughts, she kept them to herself.

Too docile, Morgan thought now. She left Arnie and approached the two young women from behind.

She strained to hear. "Yes, I think so," Karla was saying. "Sonorock is on its way out, even here in the boonies."

"Have you heard any of those Sirian groups?" Dee asked. "There's one called The Spheres. Really weird."

Morgan dropped back, relieved.

Elsie joined her. "You've got a smart guy," she said. "That Arnie, he knows which way is up. He says I can take legal action against Ahlwen now that he's made a move for Britt's money. He thinks I'd have a good swindle case."

"Not if Britt knows what she's doing."

'But that's just it. She doesn't. It's 'undue influence,' on someone who's incompetent. Temporarily deranged."

Morgan wished Arnie hadn't been so encouraging. In her opinion, Elsie ought to give up her obsession and go on with her life. "How are you going to prove anything?" she asked. "Britt may simply want the money to reinvest closer to where she's living. Maybe to start her own camp."

"Ha! Reinvest, sure. In *him!* As for proof, I'm going to get it, this trip. No more guns, no threats. She'll see me this time. She needs that signature. She'll have to talk, to convince me, and I'll get it all down on spool. Oh, I'll be a lamb, you'll see. Cool and calm. But I'll get him." She spat the last words, giving the lie to her pretense of meekness.

As Vulpius turned the line gradually north, the red and yellow of sunrise deepened into violet and lavender and muted purple. The colors, after Morgan had gazed at them for several hours, obscured for her the contours of the land. Mirages appeared. Dips and wind drifts transformed themselves into pools that fronted shimmering castles, and the occasional outcroppings of rock became crenelated towers. One such distortion, a Byzantine mosque, looked so realistic that Morgan could have sworn it was no illusion, especially when Vulpius altered course sharply to head directly for it.

Matt came swooping back. "We're to have lunch at his place. His hunting camp, he calls it. He's gone on ahead to start a fire. We just keep on straight. That's it, there. Wow! What do you think of it?"

"That you'd better save your wows. See?" The structure was already shrinking, and by the time they came up to it they saw an ordinary snowhouse built into a drift.

Inside, Vulpius had a pot of pemmican already bubbling, and a kettle of something brown and bitter that passed for tea. He stirred chunks of frozen biscuit in with the meat, and they ate squatting around the tiny stove.

The house had no comforts, only bare ice walls and a door of frozen hide. The roof was so low that Arnie and Vulpius could not stand upright, and when the seven bulky figures crouched around the stove, there was little room to spare.

Morgan contained her curiosity, but not so Arnie. "You don't *live* here, do you?" he asked.

"Naw. Place to keep supplies. To sleep sometimes. Good hunting around here."

Arnie raised his eyebrows. "Good? What do you get? I didn't see any signs of game."

"You got to look. Ergips under the snow, where it's deep. Ketsi dens. Hirvisen." His eyes disappeared in crinkles. "Even you can see *them*."

"What do you hunt with?" Matt asked.

"Here. Take a look." Vulpius backed out of the circle to a covered box next to the wall. Arnie followed, too, and the three of them bent over the cache.

Elsie tried to edge in, but there was no more space.

"He's got spears and blowers and traps," Karla said. "He made them all himself."

Elsie sniffed. "What's wrong with a gun?"

"I wouldn't expect *you* to understand."

"No, I don't," Elsie admitted. "It's why I asked."

"Just answer her question, Karla," Morgan said with a touch of asperity. "I'm curious, too. Is it because Vulpius is trying to live a completely 'natural' life?"

"Something like that," Karla said. "To kill an animal with a gun would be . . . I don't know how to say it . . ."

Dee finished for her. "A violation. I know what you mean."

"I think I do, too," Morgan said. "Everything has to be in harmony. Equal terms and no unfair advantages, with life here so hard."

Karla frowned. "It's more, too." She lowered her voice. "Uncle wouldn't admit it, but it's got a lot to do with the Argus light. With the power, and how you use it." She caught Morgan's look and stopped.

"All I know about the light is that it's given me a terrific headache," Elsie said. "It's stronger today than usual." She groped in her pocket for easetabs. "Anyone else need one?"

Morgan felt fine. "Dee?" she asked.

Dee's face, now that Morgan examined her closely, looked more pinched than usual. "I don't have a headache, exactly," she said. "Just a peculiar feeling, and there's this ringing in my ears."

"A metallic smell?" Morgan asked.

"Yes, sort of."

"It sounds like what we all get here at first. But the ringing . . . I don't know." Morgan half rose. "Arnie!"

Arnie didn't respond, and Dee pulled Morgan back. "Don't. It's really nothing." She took an easetab. "This will fix it. It's stuffy in here. I think that's all it is. I'm going outside."

Morgan followed her out, and the biting air had a restoring effect on her, too. Dee fastened on her skis and was ready to go before anyone else. She felt fine, she said. The men emerged, Vulpius closed up his house, and they were off once more.

Dee partnered with Karla again, but this time Morgan did not try to spy on them. Vulpius set a fast pace. They were still less than halfway to First Station, with five hours of skiing ahead of them.

Two weeks ago Morgan would never have believed her speed and endurance, or the ease with which she covered the miles. Two weeks ago, she thought, she had arrived in Lumisland a shivering outcast. Banished. Defeated. Now, bathed in the colors of Argus, she knew exactly what she should have said to Commander Nurmi. What she would say if she ever got the chance.

She shouldn't have let herself be cowed by him. She could have appealed to Corps Central, or merely threatened to appeal. Nurmi was insecure enough himself to have backed off. He had his career pinned to Argus Two, and wouldn't want *his* superiors to guess that there was trouble on Jaspre.

No, she knew how to manipulate Nurmi. But as she skimmed into wave after wave of radiance, Morgan wasn't sure that she wanted to leave the snows. At least not soon. If only Arnie would want to stay. He seemed to like it here, too. Matt could go to Arin's school, and Dee . . .

Morgan came back to reality with a wrench in the pit of her stomach. Dee and Karla still skied together, their heads close as they talked.

How impressionable *was* Dee? Morgan wondered. She had

always been levelheaded, but Morgan was no longer sure about anything.

Arnie was far ahead with Matt and Vulpius. She would warn him about her fears for Dee, she decided. Tonight. Not that there was much he could do except share her worry. But even that would be a help.

The wash of colors around her faded as the sky darkened. They outraced a storm that blew off into the mountains.

"Look at Argus," Elsie said.

The satellite was surrounded by two gleaming halos. The first was crimson, a perfect circle that rested on the horizon. The second was pale green, its lower third cut off by the line of the tundra. Four reflections of Argus, smaller in size but just as brilliant, appeared at equal intervals on the inner halo. Sub-arcs in soft shades of rose and green and violet dotted the outer one.

"*Jo,* she puts on a show," Vulpius said. Arnie began to explain the physics involved, the refraction and reflection and diffraction, but no one listened. Matt whooped and skied in arcs, and Morgan paid silent homage.

Karla watched quietly, too, then whispered to Dee. When Vulpius signaled for them to start off, the two young women remained together.

They arrived at First Station Lodge with the gold-streaked shades of Argus's setting. The other guests were out for the evening skiing, and the dining room was closed.

The proprietor — Karvonen, Vulpius called him — balked at providing another supper. While he and Vulpius and Arnie argued, Elsie and Morgan searched out a bath and the young people went back outside to explore the station.

Morgan waited her turn after Elsie for a hot shower that ended lukewarm, then dressed again in the same clothes. Fresh underwear was a luxury she missed, but long johns couldn't be rinsed out in a basin. Or dried overnight in a room that had ice crystals thick on the window.

She found Arnie settled in the small sitting room, warming himself at the open furzee fire. Karvonen brought coffee, and after a while Vulpius came in with Matt. "Found him in a grubber igloo, fixin' to eat dinner with the family. Purty little gal there, eh, Matt?"

Matt aimed a fist at Vulpius.

"Where are Dee and Karla?" Morgan asked.

"I wasn't, either, going to eat their food," Matt said. "It looked *awful*."

"The girls?" Morgan repeated.

"They said to tell you they'd be back later tonight," Matt began. "Dee wanted to see some camp Karla'd been telling her about. Karla said there was plenty of time before dark, and not to worry about their dinner. They'd get something to eat there."

Vulpius broke the shocked silence. "That fish brain! Magnus'll have her hide!"

Arnie looked from Morgan to Elsie. "It's that crackpot Ahlwen they've gone to see, isn't it?"

Their faces were his answer.

"Back before dark?" His accusing gaze centered on Morgan. "Then it's not as far from here as you led me to believe."

126

Morgan couldn't answer. Damn Karla, she thought. But she should have known . . .

"It's an hour on skis and snowshoes," Elsie said. "They can make it if they don't linger."

The skin around Arnie's lips was white. "After skiing for a whole day? They'll either collapse or get caught in the dark. We'd better go after them."

Vulpius shook his head. "Karla knows to stay over if she thinks they can't make it." And then he added, in an attempt to calm Arnie, "Them gals're in no danger."

"Except from *him*," Elsie said.

The lodgekeeper had been listening. "That camp's got a radio. I'll give 'em a call, if you like."

He did, and a man at Ahlwen's camp reported that Karla and Dee had already left. They would have an escort until they got back on the plain; they shouldn't be more than an hour.

It was a long wait. As Argus became a crimson slit that dyed the dark sky, the temperature plummeted rapidly. The two girls skied in under their own power, but were too tired even to unbuckle their gear.

Arnie and Morgan both assisted Dee. "That was a fool stunt," Arnie scolded. "You knew I'd say no, didn't you, if you'd asked?"

Dee did not answer.

"What happened there?" Morgan asked, dreading what she might hear. "What did you see?"

Dee pulled off her mask to reveal a strained, white face. "I'm exhausted. Can't we talk about it tomorrow?"

9

Morgan awakened before dawn to a pounding at the door.

It was Karla, carrying a candle, half dressed and frantic. "Dee's sick," she said through chattering teeth. "And I don't know what to do."

Morgan pulled on clothing without regard for buttons or laces, and Arnie struggled into his own beside her. He seized a beamer and slid into open boots, and they both followed Karla to the women's dormitory.

Dee lay on a lower bunk, half out of her sleeping bag. She tossed and moaned, feverish and incoherent.

The figures in the other bunks muttered complaints. "Let's take her to our room," Morgan whispered. She rezipped the bag, and Arnie picked up the sick girl.

Karla followed them. "She wouldn't tell me what was wrong. She was fine when we went to bed. Tired, but I was, too. We both went to sleep right away. Then, about an hour ago, I heard her and woke up."

They settled Dee in the big bed. She opened her eyes. "My head . . . the noise," she mumbled. She covered her ears with her hands.

Morgan leaned closer. "Tell me exactly: what do you feel?"

"A pressure. A ringing. Like my head is about to explode."

Arnie applied a fever patch, and it turned red. Dee kept her hands to her head and began to moan again.

"I don't suppose there's a doctor here," Arnie said.

Morgan felt the cold edge of panic. "No, not even in Satama. Unless one of the guests —"

"I'll check the register," Karla said. "And I'll wake Uncle. He'll know what to do."

None of the guests had signed as physicians, but Vulpius looked in on Dee and tried to reassure Morgan and Arnie. "Snowsickness," he said. "Seen it before, lots of times. She was out too long, that's all. A day's rest, keep the room dark, she'll be good as new." He turned to glare at Karla. "Shouldn't have happened, though. If you'd showed half the sense you was born with — What was you thinking of, anyway?"

Karla twisted her hands. "Dee wanted to go —"

"And you didn't? I heard how interested you been in that camp. Magnus shoulda kept you home." He pulled Karla out into the hall. "You done enough. Leave them alone now."

Morgan and Arnie hovered over Dee. Argus dawn lightened the room, and Morgan pinned the curtains closed.

Dee continued to thrash in her bed and suddenly blood spurted from her nose. "Arnie! Get towels, a cold pack," Morgan shouted.

Arnie ran out, and Morgan tried vainly to stanch the bleeding. "Lie still, Dee," she pleaded. Every movement of the girl's head brought another gush. Pinching her nostrils only caused her to choke, increasing the flow.

Arnie came in with towels and snow. They worked over Dee for an interminable time until the bleeding slowed to a trickle and finally stopped. Dee lay quietly, without a trace of color in her face.

Morgan rubbed Dee's cold hands and looked for another blanket. Arnie found a ragged comforter and tucked it around the top of the sleeping bag. "She seems better now," he said. "At least her fever's gone." He checked Dee's pulse and nodded. "Steady enough, but still a bit weak. Maybe after she sleeps . . ."

Dee's eyes fluttered open. "Daddy."

"I'm right here, sweetheart." He moved into her line of vision. "Don't move your head. Just keep it still."

"What did you say?"

"Not to move, sweetheart. Try to sleep now."

"Daddy, I can't hear you!"

Arnie cast a wild look at Morgan. "Try it again," she said, signaling him to conceal his agitation.

He bent over Dee and sounded his words clearly. "How is it now? Can you hear me now?"

Dee's voice shrilled with fear. "What are you saying? There's this buzzing, and I can't hear a thing!"

Arnie's face was as white as Dee's. He moved away, and Morgan replaced him by the bed. She tried to soothe Dee. "Sleep. You need to sleep." She pantomimed the word, then covered Dee's eyes with her hand.

Dee closed her eyes and snuggled into her covers like a wounded animal. Morgan stroked her head until her regular breathing indicated that she had indeed drifted off.

She joined Arnie, who was pacing by the door. "It's probably temporary. Vulpius said this sort of thing isn't unusual. She's sleeping naturally now. We'll see when she wakes up."

Arnie refused reassurance. "Vulpius! What does he know? And I'm not waiting. I'm getting Dee back to civilization as soon as I can get hold of a jetsled."

"Ask the lodgekeeper," Morgan said. "Or the snow patrol. But there's no flight out of Satama until tomorrow."

"I'll charter one." Arnie clenched a tight fist. "Damn all those doctors who said there was nothing wrong with her! And damn me for believing them!"

"Don't. You couldn't know. And it might just be the snow, after all."

He made a sound of disgust. "I'm going to check on a jetsled."

Morgan kept vigil by Dee. Matt came in with a breakfast tray. "How is she?"

"Still sleeping." Morgan took the bowl, thick porridge already cooling, and managed a few spoonfuls. "Did you get some?"

Matt grimaced. "It's all there was." He looked toward Dee again, uneasily. "She'll get better, won't she? Vulpius says it's nothing to worry about."

"He's probably right." There was no point in upsetting Matt until they knew more. Morgan returned her bowl, still nearly full, to the tray. "Thanks, but I can't eat right now." She took the cup of tea. "Where's your father?"

"Still trying to get a jetsled. He's on the phone to Satama."

Dee stirred, and they fell silent. Morgan moved to the bed.

Dee's color was better, and the new fever patch was still white. She turned over and continued to sleep.

"What can I do?" Matt asked.

Morgan knew how he must feel: disappointed and frightened and useless. She gave him a hug. "See if there's soup in the kitchen for when she wakes up. And if you see Mr. Karvonen, find out if we can get some heat in here." She glanced quickly around the room. "I guess that's all. Why don't you ask your father or Vulpius if you can go outside for a while? Just around the lodge. Ask Elsie and Karla, too. They might be able to organize something."

Matt nodded and hurried off. "Be sure to check with Arnie first," Morgan called after him. She couldn't afford to incur any more blame; her load was already too heavy.

Dee had to be all right, she prayed. She *had* to.

But when Dee awoke, she was still deaf. The pressure in her head was gone, and so were the noises. Her temperature and pulse rate were normal. She sat up with no dizziness and drank a large bowl of broth, but she couldn't hear a thing.

She was surprisingly calm, answering scribbled notes in an unmodulated but steady voice. When Arnie wrote her that he could not get a jetsled until the next day, she said not to worry. In fact, she urged everyone to go on to Second Station without her.

"No way," Arnie wrote. "We've all had enough of this fool trek. Of this whole place. We're taking you back with us to Friishaven."

Dee didn't respond. Instead, she asked to see Karla.

Arnie shook his head.

"Please," she begged.

Arnie looked at Morgan, but she refused to help him out. Dee appealed again, and finally he relented. "It can't do any harm now," he said. "I'll get her."

Arnie left, and Morgan regarded Dee uneasily. Someone in her condition should be frightened, perhaps even in tears, instead of so strangely composed.

Morgan reached for the pad. "What's on your mind?" she wrote. "What are you planning?"

"Nothing at all," Dee said. Her voice was a too-loud monotone. "I like Karla. She'll help me pass the time."

Morgan sat with Dee until Karla came. The room was still darkened, but Morgan had tidied it and found a table to place beside the bed. Karvonen had brought in a portable stove, and Matt had made a snow cat that sat on the table and dripped slowly into a bowl.

Karla came in and stood hesitantly by the bed. Even in the dim light Morgan could see that she had been crying.

"You can leave us alone," Dee said.

Morgan found Arnie by the sitting room fire, talking to Vulpius. "I'm tellin' you, I've seen it before," Vulpius was saying. "It lasts a day, then it's gone."

"And have they been deaf, like Dee?" Arnie's voice was sharply impatient.

Vulpius scratched his head. "That's what's puzzlin'. Some

133

of the others was snowblind, though. Took a while longer, but they got over it. I still say, wait a bit. You get back to Friisland and the little gal's okay, you'll be sorry you rushed off."

"But what if she isn't okay?" Morgan said. "I agree with Arnie: we can't afford to take the chance."

Vulpius shrugged. "Just tellin' you what I think." He mopped his face. "Too hot in here. I'll be out with the boy. Promised to show him how to make a snowhouse." He left.

Arnie's face was bleak. "Why did we ever come here?"

Morgan's guilt lay heavy again. "We'd better go check on the girls," she said. There was no telling what might be transpiring in the room.

The bed and table were littered with notes, and Karla was still scribbling. "Yes, I'm sure," Dee was saying in her flat voice. "I know he can do it." When she saw Morgan and Arnie, she clasped her hands. "You've got to get him," she begged. "Anders Ahlwen. Karla says he'll come, and I know he can cure me."

Though Morgan had expected something of the sort, she had no ready reply.

Arnie answered for them both. "Never!" he shouted. A crimson flush rose from his neck. "That crackpot quack isn't coming anywhere near you. What went on, anyway, at that camp yesterday? It's his fault, you know, that you're in the condition you are. If you hadn't gone there —"

Dee held up her hands and shook her head. Arnie's flush deepened as he seized a paper and printed a single block-lettered "NO."

Dee poked Karla. "Tell him."

Karla glanced uneasily at Arnie. "It's true, he can do it." She twined white-knuckled fingers. "He's healed lots of people; it's a fact. I've even seen it on holos that I know weren't faked. He's at his camp now. We saw him there last night and talked to him. He liked Dee, and I know if we got him on the radio he'd come right away."

"Get out," Arnie said. "I was a fool to let you near Dee again."

Karla started to leave but hesitated.

Arnie took a step toward her. "Did you hear me?"

Karla gave Dee a stricken look and edged out the door.

"Morgan?" Dee said.

Morgan tried to think of what to do, how to help Dee without alienating Arnie. But while she paused, Arnie spoke for her again. "Morgan has nothing to do with this," he wrote. Then he printed carefully: "I'm taking you to a *real* doctor, and no more nonsense. No more seeing Karla. She's bad for you. This whole place is bad for you. Tomorrow we'll be out of here for good, back to Friishaven." He added a scrawled "I love you."

Dee held the note. "Morgan," she repeated, pleading.

Morgan fought conflicting emotions. Deliver Dee to Ahlwen? They couldn't. She agreed with Arnie. But yet — what if he *could* cure her? She only wanted what was best for Dee, and maybe it was worth the risk.

She turned to Arnie. "I don't know, maybe with all of us here to watch him . . . what could we lose?"

"Our sanity, if you seriously expect me to invite that con man here." Red mottled his face again. "You heard what Elsie said. God, you've *been* there. Whatever is going on

135

with you, Morgan, I don't get it. I'm even wondering whose side you're on."

"I'm on *Dee's* side, of course. I thought we all were!" As Morgan's anger rose, words that she had not intended spilled out. "I'm wondering about you, too. How far you're prepared to go before that pride of yours cracks. Before you're willing to admit that there may be *something* — I don't say total truth, just a possibility of something we don't understand — in what Karla and Dee and a lot of other unprejudiced people have found here. Have found in Ahlwen."

Arnie stared as if at a stranger. "He's gotten to you, too."

"No! I just said 'maybe.' That it's worth a chance."

Dee had been looking from one to the other. She left her bed and crossed the floor to Arnie. "Please," she said. She plucked at his arm. "Please, Daddy."

He steered her back to the bed and found a blank paper. "It's been settled," he wrote. "No more visitors at all."

He showed the note to Morgan. "Dee's leaving tomorrow, and until then she's to be alone with no one but me. Not Karla, not Matt, not even you. I'm sorry, but I can't trust anyone. Not any longer. Now go find the lodgekeeper and get a key to this room. When I'm not here, it'll be locked."

"You think she'd try to get away?"

"You mentioned chances. I'm not taking any."

Arnie had once been a SEF security chief. Dee would be well guarded, Morgan knew.

Perhaps too well. As she searched for Karvonen, she muttered against Arnie's stubbornness, marshaling arguments that she knew she would never use.

The trouble was, she wasn't at all sure that Arnie wasn't

right. Ahlwen might be able to heal Dee — but at what price? On the one hand Morgan saw Dee's pleading eyes, and on the other, Britt Halsemer's, gleaming with the light of fanaticism. She saw Dee shouting, "I can't hear!" and Britt sitting in a freezing cell, preparing herself for a suicidal journey.

If only Vulpius were right. If she could believe that Dee would be well in the morning, she could stop torturing herself with suppositions. If only . . . Morgan almost ran into Elsie, coming in from outside.

The snow-dusted woman lifted her goggles. "Talking to yourself, Morgan? A bad sign." She peered closer. "What's wrong? Is Dee worse?"

"No, she's better, but she still can't hear. Arnie —" Morgan stopped. She knew she would get no help from Elsie, who would support Arnie completely. "Arnie's with Dee now," she finished. "I'm looking for our host. Have you seen him?"

"No, I've been gone all morning. I just got back from Ahlwen's camp." Elsie shrugged out of her parka. "I've got to talk to Arnie."

"Go on up to the room. I'll be there as soon as — oh, there's Karvonen now. Tell Arnie I'll be up with the key."

The lodgekeeper grumbled as he rummaged through a cluttered drawer. "Foolishness. Nothin's been stole from a room in twenty years." He dragged out a ring of rusted keys. "One of them'll fit. You try them."

Morgan found Arnie and Elsie standing outside the door of Dee's room. "She was so distant," Elsie was saying. "So cold. As if I were nothing but a business partner. She offered to buy out my share of everything, and when I refused she said she'd force a sale." She turned to Morgan. "Britt's completely changed." To Arnie: "And you're right about Dee. If Ahlwen's got a hold on her already, don't let him get anywhere near her. The man's a magnet. You'll never believe who I ran into at his camp — part of that bunch who flew in with you. The ones who came straight on here in the jetsled. They went to see *him*. There they were, in and out of all the tunnels, oohing and ahing and sucking up the line of mystic claptrap those 'disciples' were putting out. I skied back with them, and I've never heard such drivel."

"Did you see Ahlwen?" Morgan asked.

"No, and it's probably a good thing. I kept my temper with Britt, even when she threatened legal action against *me*. But I don't think I could have done it if I'd come face to face with that crooked slimeball faker." She turned back to Arnie. "I let Britt do a lot of talking, and I got it all down. So where do I go from here?"

Arnie had tried the keys and found the right one. "Let me think about it." He looked in on Dee, then locked the door. "I promised to get her something to read. And I'll pick up lunch for both of us. Isn't it about that time?" He addressed Elsie, deliberately ignoring Morgan.

Morgan said nothing to him, either. The three of them went down to the dining room, where Matt and Vulpius were already eating. The other guests, the skiers Elsie had returned with from Ahlwen's camp, were there, too, and the room was loud with voices and clatter.

They served themselves from a buffet. Arnie filled a tray for himself and Dee, continuing to ignore Morgan.

138

She seated herself beside Vulpius. So now she was the enemy, she thought, angry and hurt. Vulpius gave her an odd look. Matt, chattering away to Vulpius and one of the new arrivals about his snowhouse project, gave little notice to anything else.

Arnie did not remain long in the dining room. He put down his tray to exchange a few words with Matt, and again to speak even more briefly to an acquaintance from the plane. The next time Morgan looked for him he was gone.

Morgan had little appetite for the hirvisen roast or the reconstituted greens. Voices rose around her, isolating her in walls of sound. She thought of Arnie, imprisoned in his stubbornness, and Dee, in her silence.

She felt Karla looking at her from the next table and imagined what she was thinking: that she should have stood up against Arnie. Karla was so sure she was right. Just as Arnie was.

Vulpius was sure, too. Everyone knew what was best for Dee, but she was legally an adult. Morgan hadn't been seeing her as one either, she had to admit. Maybe it was time she changed.

Morgan gave up pushing her food around and offered it to Matt. She couldn't stand the inaction. She decided to go see Arnie and Dee, to see if Arnie would soften any.

She got as far as the hall before she changed her mind. "I can't trust anyone," Arnie had said. "Not even you." He probably wouldn't even let her in.

Matt came out of the dining room. "Will you come out and see the snowhouse, Mom?" he asked.

She agreed and spent an hour in the drifts behind the

rock spires, helping him and Vulpius shape the roof and entrance. The man and the boy had piled up and tramped a mound of snow as high as Matt himself and had dug out the interior. The curving walls became reflecting mirrors of Argus when they were smoothed and polished, and Matt worked with furious energy.

Morgan was happy to see him occupied, but her own worries drove her back to the lodge.

It was quiet inside, the morning skiers apparently all resting before going out again. She tried Dee's door, but it was locked. She knocked and called softly, then more loudly, but no one answered.

Arnie would hardly be napping. No, he still didn't want to see her, Morgan decided. She continued on to the women's dormitory, though she knew she was too keyed up to sleep.

As she expected, it was futile. Her own sleeping bag was in the other room, and the one she found smelled rank and musty. Elsie and another woman snored, and someone else coughed.

Morgan rolled herself into a tight ball and clasped her arms. Why would Arnie lock the door from inside? Perhaps he had just stepped out. She decided to try again in half an hour.

She gave in before then. Back at the locked door, she pounded and shouted and even kicked. Arnie couldn't be inside and not respond. But neither would he leave Dee alone for so long.

She ran in search of Karvonen. There had to be another key.

"*Voi kahistus,*" the lodgekeeper muttered. He pulled open drawers and slammed them shut. "Never again! Didn't need no key in the first place, told you so. Now — no, there ain't another one." He straightened and glared. "What's goin' on in there, anyway? Who's locked you out?"

"My daughter's sick in there. She can't hear, and I'm afraid something may have happened. Have you got a file — a screwdriver? We've got to get that door open."

The old man continued to grumble, but Morgan's urgency overcame his reluctance. They couldn't budge the lock, and he refused to break it. Finally they took the door off by the hinges.

Arnie lay slumped over the bedside table, deep in a drugged stupor. Dee was gone.

10

"You try to wake him," Morgan cried. "I've got to find Dee!" She ran to check the ski rack and discovered Dee's space empty. Her parka and boots were missing, too.

It wasn't hard to figure where she had gone. Morgan tried to control her panic. She bundled up quickly and hurried outside to get Vulpius.

He was still working with Matt on the snowhouse, though clouds darkened the sky and it had grown considerably colder. "Is Karla gone, too?" he asked at once.

Morgan had been too distraught to notice. They checked the skis again, and Karla's were there. Only three pairs were missing — Dee's and those of a couple who had left early in the morning for Second Station.

"She's gone to Ahlwen's camp," Morgan said. "I know it. But she could never find her way alone."

"I'll look for tracks," Vulpius said. "You find out who helped her. Get it out of Karla. She's gotta know about this."

Matt looked, frightened, from one to the other. "But I thought . . . you said . . . why would she run off like that?"

"I can't explain it now," Morgan said. "You want to help? Go see who's in the men's dorm. Tell them to get out here, that it's important."

Morgan hurried to rouse the women.

The guests assembled in the entry hall, grumbling and shivering. Morgan could find out nothing. No one had seen Dee leave or noticed anyone tampering with Arnie's food. Karla stoutly affirmed her innocence, maintaining, "If you'd done what she wanted, and let Ahlwen come here, this wouldn't have happened."

Vulpius came in. "She lit out for the mountains all right. Someone joined her just beyond the station. Two pairs of tracks goin' east. Least she's not alone," he added for what comfort it was. "Want me to take you to the camp? It might be better to wait, though. Weather don't look too good."

"No, we'll go right away," Morgan said. "As soon as I see how Arnie is." She dismissed the others with an apology for having disturbed them.

They dispersed, all except Matt and Elsie and Vulpius. "Ahlwenites!" Elsie snorted. "Any one of them could have slipped Arnie a powder. Someone put them up to it, though. You — Karla!" she called. "Come back here."

The girl returned.

"You were sitting with that bunch at lunch. I suppose you did a lot of talking?"

Karla held herself stiffly. "No more than usual."

"About Dee?"

"So what if I did! I have a right to my opinions, and no one can keep me from saying what I think."

"And have you been talking on the radio, too?"

"No! I don't know what you're getting at."

"At who came to meet Dee, and how they knew about it."

"I told you before. I didn't do anything!"

"It doesn't matter now, Elsie," Morgan said. "We can't waste time on that." She waved Karla away.

"I'll get the gear ready," Vulpius said.

Morgan and Elsie started for Arnie's room. "Matt, you stay down here," Morgan said.

"No, I want to see Dad."

Morgan gave in but stopped the boy outside the door. "Wait here, just for a minute."

Arnie was sitting up and shaking his wet head while Karvonen splashed him with water from a basin. "Knew that'd wake him," the old man said with a grin.

Arnie groaned.

Morgan handed him a towel. "How do you feel? Do you know what happened?"

"Something in the coffee. I thought it tasted worse than usual. I went out like a light." He looked around slowly. "Dee?" Comprehension dawned. "She's gone, hasn't she? They've kidnapped her, that snow-crazy cult!"

Matt came in, his eyes wide. "Dee's been kidnapped?"

"No, she apparently went willingly," Morgan said. "Though she had help." She watched Arnie anxiously as he struggled to his feet. "If you feel well enough — Vulpius and I are going after her."

144

"Of course I'm coming," Arnie said. "I'll drag her out of there, and I'll crack a few heads while I'm doing it!" He paced slowly, weaving a bit, to the door and back to the table. He eyed the basin. "Is that good water?"

Karvonen nodded, and Arnie drank noisily. "Ah!" He wiped his mouth. "That did it. I'm ready to go."

His eyes were clear, and if he felt any further distress he concealed it.

"Me too," Matt said. "I'll get my stuff."

Morgan grabbed the boy's arm. "Hold on. You're not going anywhere." She turned to Elsie. "You'll stay with him, won't you?"

"Not me," Elsie said. "I'm going to watch Arnie crack those heads."

"I can keep up, Dad. Please let me go," Matt wheedled.

Arnie turned from pulling on a dry sweater. "No! And no arguments. Karvonen, you keep an eye on him. See that he stays inside until we're back."

The lodgekeeper started to grumble. Arnie barked, "Put it on the bill!" and Karvonen subsided. Matt sulked.

Morgan zipped herself into her layers of outside gear. Vulpius was waiting with her skis and a light pack. "Good," he said of Arnie and Elsie. "More the better. Don't know how friendly they'll be."

Elsie took the lead, followed by Arnie, Morgan, and then Vulpius. The weather was still threatening, with a knife-cold wind and shifting clouds. When Argus shone, even against the wind they made fair progress. Under a dark sky, they labored.

Dee would have found it hard going in her weakened

condition. Morgan hoped that she had gotten away early, before the wind came up.

She worried about Arnie, too. He was skiing in a mechanical fashion, his masked face staring straight ahead, his arms and legs moving with robotlike rigidity.

She sped up to join him. "Are you sure you're all right?" she asked.

He swerved away from her. "I'm fine." He didn't turn his head.

She knew it wasn't true, but there was nothing she could do since he obviously wanted to be left alone. She fell back into line and tried not to think about what they might find at the camp.

When they changed to snowshoes, Arnie still would not talk to her. He hadn't said that he blamed her, but she was sure he did. You knew about Karla, she imagined him thinking. You knew about this camp.

Arnie was armed with his service lasgun. Would it be a match for Ahlwen's power? she wondered.

Elsie thought so. "That smart-ass guru's met his match this time," she chortled to Morgan. "I can't wait!"

They started off again, with Elsie once more in the lead. The clouds thickened, and snow fell. Morgan had to clear her goggles constantly. She struggled to negotiate the up and down drifts on the clumsy footgear, and after a stop to adjust clamps she lost sight of Arnie.

Vulpius caught up with her. "Crazy fools're goin' too fast," he complained. "They're supposed to wait for us."

They were in the region of precipitous cliffs and ravines

that led into Ahlwen's enclave. "It must be close now, I think," Morgan said.

Vulpius consulted a map and his compass, then looked around for landmarks. He nodded and pointed. "*Jo,* we're goin' the right way." Directly ahead and below them Morgan recognized the narrow gully that ran like a gash between wings of snow. Two small figures moved about halfway along its length.

Morgan and Vulpius started down.

"Wait." Vulpius stopped her. He removed his goggles and squinted at a spot on the cliff. "Someone's up there."

"There are guards all around," Morgan said. She followed his gaze. The sky was dark, and through the falling snow she saw a flash of light. Then she heard a rumbling as a portion of the cliff broke off and fell into the ravine.

"Arnie!" Morgan screamed. The scene below was a white haze, and it was impossible to distinguish detail.

With Vulpius beside her, Morgan half scrambled, half slid into the gully. Trying to run, she tripped over her snowshoes and fell. Clumsy boats! She struggled to her feet and ran again.

Vulpius was at the slide before her, climbing over the mountain of snow. He stopped and waved, shouting. "He's all right!"

Morgan crawled to the top. Vulpius and Arnie were digging frantically. "Elsie!" Arnie gasped. "She's in there!"

There was too much snow to move. They dug until they themselves were buried and had to haul one another out. It seemed hopeless.

There was no sign of the figures on the cliff top. "We'd better get help from the camp," Morgan said.

"You two go," Vulpius said. "I'll keep trying to find her."

"Come on," Morgan urged Arnie. "I know the way from here."

Soft avalanche snow blocked the passage for as far as Morgan could see. They floundered over it, falling repeatedly and losing their snowshoes. Finally they discarded them and waded, knee-deep and hip-deep.

They struggled for a hundred yards, then another before they were back on firmer footing. Ahead of them lay the entrance tunnel to Ahlwen's camp.

Morgan plodded woodenly. Snow had gotten into her gloves, and she couldn't feel her hands. Her face mask was stiff with ice.

Guards came. "Back there." Arnie pointed. "There's a woman buried in the snow."

Shouts brought more shaggy-coated figures out of the tunnel. Two pulled a sled loaded with rescue equipment.

"At the other end of the slide," Arnie said. "There's a man there who'll show you where to dig."

"Come inside." A guard with a woman's voice beckoned. "You can't go back there now, either of you."

She led Morgan and Arnie into the cave. Morgan felt herself swaying, and she saw Arnie stumble. They went through a short passageway into a room with a furze stove.

The woman helped Morgan remove her gloves and mask, which were frozen, the mask stuck to her face. Her fingers were white and hard.

Morgan extended her hands to the fire, but the woman

pulled them away. She guided them under her parka and through an opening in her bodysuit to smooth flesh that radiated a feverish warmth.

Morgan gasped. She felt a tingling in her hands and then sharp stabs, but the pain was bearable. Soon it became an exquisite sensation. Her fingers became a conduit for a warming current that coursed through her arms to her entire chilled body.

When Morgan withdrew her hands, they were pink and healthy. She showed them to Arnie, who was bent over the stove. "They were half frozen," she said. "Let her —"

"No!" he barked. He continued to rub his own hands and cheeks. "Have you forgotten why we're here?" He lowered his voice so only Morgan could hear. "I wouldn't trust any of them near me. You'd better be careful, too. If you ask me, that avalanche was no accident."

Arnie turned from the fire and addressed the female guard. "We're looking for a young woman who must have come here within the last two or three hours. She was here last night, too. She's been ill, and her hearing has been affected. Her name is Dee Vernor, and we're her parents."

"Ah, yes." The woman pushed back her hood. She was young, not much older than Dee, Morgan guessed. Her face was snow-browned, but she was not a grubber. She smiled. "We all liked Dee a lot. You mustn't worry about her. She's quite well now. Anders healed her himself."

Arnie made an explosive sound with his breath. "I want to see her."

"I'm afraid that isn't possible. She isn't here."

Morgan stepped forward. "You mean she's gone back

to the station?" Fear seized her. "How long ago? She wasn't . . . ? That avalanche . . ."

"No, no. I told you not to worry. She's gone north to one of the other camps. She left a letter for you. Wait here and I'll get it."

"I'll go with you," Arnie said. His face was set as hard as if it were still snow-bitten. "I don't believe she's not here. I won't, until I've seen every inch of this place. And I want to talk to this man Ahlwen."

The young woman hesitated. "He isn't here now, either. And I don't know if I can let you into the living quarters. I'll have to ask."

"Do that. But I'm going to search, anyway."

Arnie strode from the room, with the woman after him. "Please," she begged. "If you'll just read the letter first. I'll be back with it in a minute."

"And while we're waiting, you can hide Dee. No, I'm not falling for that. I'm looking for her now." He continued out into the passageway, which connected with the main arterial tunnel. The guard and Morgan followed at his heels, half running to match his pace.

"Dee! Are you in here, Dee?" Arnie shouted. He came to a room opening and pulled aside the curtain.

It was a four-bed sleeping room, empty. "Check the rooms on the other side," he directed Morgan.

The guard ran down the tunnel. "Intruders!" she shrieked. "Toivo! Ilmi!" She called other names. "I need help!"

Morgan hung back, unsure what to do. Angry men and women filled the tunnel.

A wrinkled old man with thin white hair and a wispy

beard confronted her. "What's going on here?" he demanded. "Who gave you leave to come in?" His eyes were pinpoints of cold blue ice that immobilized her, so that she was unable even to speak. Arnie, she saw, was similarly held.

He released Morgan first. "We're looking for someone," she said. "Our daughter."

"I told them to wait," the woman guard said. "Ilmi, give them the letter."

A young grubber woman handed a sealed paper to Morgan. Arnie, released from his paralysis, joined her to read it.

Morgan broke the seal. "Dear Dad and Morgan," she read. "I know you are going to be upset when you get this, but please try not to be angry with me. I have found something that is right for me, and if you love me you will understand and wish me well.

"First of all, I can hear again, and I feel stronger than I have since I left New Terra — or even before that. It is all due to Anders Ahlwen. He has wonderful powers, and he thinks I can learn them, too. The people in his camp all love him, and there is the greatest, warmest feeling here.

"We have a mission that will help everyone on the planet, and I want to be part of it. I *will* see you again, but I don't know exactly when. I'm going to another camp with Anders and some of my new friends. It is a place that does not allow visitors, so please don't try to follow me.

"Again, I'm fine and I'm happy. I feel *complete,* Morgan. I've finally found what I was searching for. Please don't worry about me, Daddy. I love you both. Dee."

It was clearly Dee's writing, even to the curly-tailed cat she drew into her signature.

Arnie studied it and agreed. "Though they could have made her write it," he said in an undertone to Morgan. "Like that white-haired guy did to us. It wouldn't be hard for them to force Dee."

"But what if the letter is genuine?" Morgan asked.

"Then they've suckered her." He gave Morgan a quick, suspicious glance. "Maybe you, too. That sweetness and love baloney. It smacks of Astran cultism. And those 'missions.' You've seen them before. A lot of cash gets collected, and it all goes into one pocket. No, I don't buy it." He raised his voice and spoke to the others. "You're not taking me in with this." He crumpled the letter and tossed it to Morgan. "I still want to search the rest of the camp."

"Toivo?" someone asked.

The old man shrugged. "Ilmi, take him through." He regarded Morgan with a hint of a smile. "You, do you want to look, too, for our hidden prisoner?"

"Yes, of course I do," Morgan said. Dee wasn't a prisoner, she was fairly sure of it, but she might well be participating in a deception to elude them. She refolded the letter and placed it in an inside pocket.

Ilmi shepherded Morgan and Arnie through the entire complex — some two dozen sleeping rooms and work-rooms, a central kitchen and dining hall and sanitary facility, and the hydro garden Morgan had glimpsed on her visit with Elsie.

Everyone willingly vacated rooms so they could search. They interrupted children at their lessons, adults involved in vigorous dance-exercise sessions, work groups producing what looked like salable items of weaving and beadwork, and countless solitary meditations.

They found no trace of Dee. "Are you satisfied?" Ilmi asked as she led them back to the entrance.

Arnie grunted. "Where is this other camp?" he asked.

"I couldn't tell you even if I knew."

"A secret hideaway, eh? Well, you can let your leader know that I'll find it, and I'll find Dee, and there's no way he can stop me."

In the entrance cave, Vulpius was waiting alone. "What about the gal?" he asked at once. "Did you get to see her?"

"No, we were too late," Morgan said. "They've taken her away." She saw a covered form on the rescue sled and smothered a cry.

"*Jo,* it's Elsie," Vulpius said. "She was dead when we found her."

Arnie uncovered the face and swore softly.

"Did you tell him what we saw on the ridge?" Vulpius asked Morgan.

"No, not yet." Arnie looked up, and she told him about the guard and the light flash. "Perhaps it was a warning about the loose snow."

"Ha! More likely it was someone starting the avalanche deliberately, with a laser blast. Delaying us. I wouldn't even be surprised if Elsie was the target. She was making too much trouble for them."

"Surely not!" Arnie, Morgan felt, was way off base. "Snowslides happen out here all the time. Elsie was just unlucky."

Arnie shook his head stubbornly. "No. With her dead, the cult gets her whole estate. Did you see that former friend of hers anywhere?"

"I didn't, and you know, it's odd." Morgan called back Ilmi, who was returning inside. "Where is Britt Halsemer? Someone had better get her."

"Britt went with Dee and Anders," Ilmi said. She glared at Arnie. "Your accusations — they are ridiculous."

Arnie started to reply, but Vulpius held up his hand. "They said we can use the sled to take the body out. Might as well get goin', if you're through here."

"Let's go, then," Arnie said. "I've another trip ahead of me."

Outside, two guards helped them drag the sled over the avalanche snow. When they were alone again and on their way, Vulpius asked Arnie about his plans. "Didn't want you to say too much front o' them back there. If they thought we was dangerous, we might never make it to the station."

Arnie stopped pulling the sled. He looked back in the direction of Ahlwen's camp, then down at Elsie's body. He raised both his arms. "Murderers!" he shouted. His voice echoed along the ravine. "Now that I know what they're like, I'm going to find Dee no matter what it costs me. And as for that pervert Ahlwen — I swear to God I'll kill him!"

11

Back at First Station, in the lodge dining room, Morgan found Arnie and Vulpius busy with maps and charts when she returned from seeing Matt off to bed.

"Ahlwen's got a camp here, about thirty miles northeast of Third Station," Vulpius was saying. "I can get a sled in the morning and we'll go there first, but I don't think they'll be there."

"Why not?" Arnie asked.

"Too close. Too easy to find. If he's hidin' the gal, they'll be up on the glacier. He's supposed to have a place there. Varma, I've heard it called, but nobody I know's ever seen it. From what Dee said in that letter, that's where they're headin'."

Morgan leaned over the table to study the map of Lumisland. The larger, northern part of the continent was uncharted, marked only as stretches of glacial ice. She traced it with her finger. "Here there be dragons," she murmured.

"What's that?" Arnie looked up with a frown.

"It's what cartographers used to put on ancient maps, where no one had explored. Vulpius, how will we ever find this camp?"

"I got ways."

"Vulpius is a skilled tracker," Arnie said. "But there's no 'we' as far as you're concerned, Morgan. You know you can't go with us."

"I don't know any such thing! Why not?"

"Matt, for starters. Your job. And according to Vulpius, that glacier's a killer. It's got whiteouts and blinding storms and crusted-over pits that'll swallow you. Not to mention the crazies. It's no place for you."

Morgan had her answers ready. "Matt can go back to Satama on the sled tomorrow, and Arin will put him on the plane to Friishaven. I'm going to call Jazmin tonight. I'm sure he can stay with her until we get back. My job's a lost cause anyway, and as for the glacier — you know perfectly well how tough I am."

"I have other reasons. You know what they are."

She felt heat flare in her cheeks. "I don't. Suppose you share them with me."

Vulpius glanced from one to the other. "I'll be out there, checkin' the gear." He beat a fast retreat.

Morgan stared levelly at Arnie. "You can't keep me out of this. I'm as concerned about Dee as you are. And she and I have a rapport that will work a lot better, if we find her, than your cave-man tactics of dragging her away by force."

"Rapport!" Arnie snorted derisively. "That's what I meant.

The time for talking is over. I don't want anyone with me who's soft on Ahlwen."

"You think I am?"

"I know it." He stared back at her, unwavering. "It's your fault she's in this mess. You knew what was going on up here. You and Karla both. Take you along, to warn Dee and protect the man who's holding her? I'd have to be crazy!"

Morgan gasped and started to defend herself, but he cut her off. "I meant what I said about finding Ahlwen and killing him. You can run back to SEF and get a squadron out to track me down, but it won't do you any good. He's going to pay for what he's done to Dee. There's one thing I've always been able to do, and that's take care of my family."

Arnie was over the edge, Morgan saw. Nevertheless, she tried to reason. "You know you can't take justice into your own hands."

"I can when I can't get it any other way. You've meddled enough, Morgan. Quit now."

"Is that a threat?"

"Just don't try to come after me."

Anger and frustration welled up in Morgan and she stormed from the room, half blinded by tears.

She collided with Vulpius. "Didn't work, eh?" the grubber said. "Thought you was wastin' your time."

Morgan focused her anger on him. "Why are you helping him? You know the state he's in. Does the pay mean so much to you that you'd guide a madman bent on murder? What's going to happen to Arnie if he carries out his threats? Have you even thought about that?"

"*Jo,* I've done a lot of thinkin'. About your gal and about Karla. I've thought it's time someone gets rid of Anders Ahlwen before he's poisoned all our young folks."

"So you'll take Arnie up there and let him do your dirty work."

"God knows if we'll even find the place. I ain't been on that ice for years. We'll be lucky if either of us makes it back."

"You're as mad as he is!" There was no point in talking to him, either. Morgan watched him rejoin Arnie, then crossed the hall and walked into the sitting room.

As she paced before the fire, her anger dissipated but not the cold pressure of her fear. Arnie's course could end in nothing but disaster. Unlike him and Vulpius, Morgan could not conceive of Dee's being in any immediate danger. She'd been brainwashed, perhaps. Maybe touched by whatever powers Argus might after all have. But physically she was safe, Morgan was sure of it.

She pulled out Dee's letter and read it again. "I have found something that is right for me. . . . I'm going to another camp . . . a place that does not allow visitors . . ."

Ahlwen's camps were well guarded. Vulpius knew what they were getting into. If Arnie made good his threats, he might never return.

And there would be no dissuading him. Arnie had always been unwavering when he thought himself right and fiercely protective where his family was concerned. When the twins were little he had wiped noses, cooked hot meals along with Morgan, and struggled to keep them in shoes. After Dee's accident he had sat by her bed for days, all of it part of the caring quality that Morgan had loved in him.

She squeezed her arms until they ached. She had to save Arnie somehow. She had to find Dee before Arnie could exact his bloody revenge. She would hire her own guides and make her own way to the glacier camp as soon as Arnie left and she could see Matt safely off.

She made two radio calls, both successful. Arin agreed to book Matt a plane seat, and Jazmin said that Matt was welcome to stay with her until either Morgan or Arnie returned.

She had intended to ask Karvonen about guides, but changed her mind when she saw him in conversation with Arnie and Vulpius. Better to wait, she thought. When it was safe, she was sure she could bribe him.

Arnie did not come to their room. If he slept at all, it was elsewhere. Morgan shivered through the night in the big bed and arose at first light to find the two men already gone.

The passengers for Satama boarded the sled after breakfast. Morgan saw them off, Matt huddled glumly in the seat beside Karla. "Dad didn't even say goodbye," he said with a catch in his voice.

"He did, but you were asleep," Morgan lied.

Matt believed it, and his face lost some of its tightness. "You'll find them, won't you? Dad and Dee?"

There was no need to tell him the story she had prepared; he knew why she had to stay. She gave him a last hug and stepped back as the sled powered up. It glided off smoothly on runners cased with ice.

At the lodge, Morgan had a visitor. "He come just after you left," Karvonen said. "He's waitin' out back. Says it's too hot for him in here." The lodgekeeper ushered her through the kitchen and out the side door to a rickety porch. A figure in grubber furs stood at the rail.

"Toivo!" Morgan recognized the white-haired old man from Ahlwen's camp.

"You know him?" Karvonen regarded the other man suspiciously.

"Yes, it's all right," Morgan said. Karvonen, shivering in a thick sweater, went back inside.

Morgan's heart began to beat wildly. "What are you doing here? Is it something about Dee — or Arnie?"

Toivo held up his hand. "*Rauha.* Calm yourself. The girl is safe. Your husband is, too, as far as I know. Though it's because of him I came."

"What do you mean?"

"Your husband is in great danger. Yesterday, when you left the camp, some of our men heard what he said, that he would kill Anders. Rantings, we thought, but all the same I came here to check. I find he's already gone. And with Vulpius, he might be unlucky enough to find Varma. It's guarded by the *elukka miehet,* the beast men. Poor creatures crazed by Argus. Someone will be hurt up there, and it won't be one of us."

Morgan swallowed. "What . . . why have you come to me?"

"Maybe you can stop him. We don't want any more deaths. The Tersteegen woman was bad enough. That was a sad

accident, and Anders — all of us — agree that it has to
the last."

Morgan studied him, wondering if she could trust him. It
was almost too lucky, his showing up just when she needed
a guide. She avoided his eyes, suspecting they could make
her believe anything.

"We can overtake him," Toivo said. "I can travel fast.
Much faster than Vulpius."

She stalled. "And what happens if we do find him? You
won't be able to change his purpose. And he won't listen to
me, either."

"If we could get to your daughter first. Then, if she would
meet with her father, talk to him —"

"Yes," Morgan agreed. "It might work."

"We have to hurry," he urged. "If he gets to the camp
before us, those half-minded beasts will tear him apart. I
have a powersled over there, behind the lodge, and everything we need for the glacier. Can you go now?"

Since she had already accepted, she looked into his eyes.

There was no guile. She knew his fear and his terrible
urgency. "Yes, I'm ready," she said.

12

The wall of ice towered a hundred, a thousand, two thousand feet. At the top it leveled into a plateau that went on beyond the limits of Morgan's vision, gleaming in brilliant, cold colors, a mantle that covered a quarter of the planet, extending into the unimaginable frozen distances of the north.

The face was a sheer cliff for two hundred or more feet, then it sloped into a jumble of icy ridges and huge up-jutting blocks from which Argus light danced and gleamed.

Thoroughly impassable, Morgan thought.

Toivo pointed to the west. "We're off course a bit. There's an opening there, an easy way up."

They pushed off again on their skis. Toivo had left his sled at Ahlwen's Third Station camp, where they had spent the night. Their food and equipment were now in their backpacks. Varma was a two-day journey, and they would spend only one night on the ice. "We usually pull sleds and bring in supplies," Toivo said. "But that would add another day. Vulpius will be traveling light, too."

They had found out at the camp that Arnie and Vulpius were ahead of them, but Toivo wasn't worried. "He'll be looking for tracks to Varma, and that'll slow him down."

Morgan's breath was a white cloud around her face mask, with crystals of ice at her nose and mouth. She wore grubber outer clothing, tightly sewn hirvisen fur that insulated heat and repelled moisture. Her hands were protected with fingerless woolen mitts under full mittens, and she had ketsiskin overgloves tied to her parka with a cord. It had been thirty degrees below freezing when they left the camp, and Toivo said it would be colder on the glacier.

They skied over soft new snow for half an hour, the glacier towering over them, until they came to a break in the cliff. A great tongue of ice cut through the jumbled walls, offering a clear passage all the way up to the plateau.

They started up slowly, roped together, with skins on their skis for traction. Toivo went first, probing with his poles for snow-covered pits or fissures. They encountered none, and when they finally leveled off after a two-hour climb, they were beyond the treacherous area of the rim.

Toivo untied the rope. "Up here the surface is safe," he said. "We can make better time." A light snow obscured Argus. Ahead, Morgan could see nothing but a vast, featureless icescape that dissolved into a chilled haze.

Toivo started off and waved for her to follow. For all his apparent years, he moved with the vigor of a young man. He appeared as eager as she to reach Varma before Arnie, and Morgan told herself that she had done well to trust herself to him.

They skied over an ever-changing terrain, now flat, now

rising and falling. A wind followed them and eased their way. In the high places it scoured away the new-fallen snow, and they sped over slick ice with a flick of their poles. In other areas, the compacted snow was windblown into solid drifts. Here they skirted and climbed, and Morgan's pack began to weigh heavily. Toivo glanced back frequently at the curtain that hid Argus, and she could guess his thoughts. She, too, longed for the energizing light.

They struggled on for an hour, then another as the wind changed and blew from the north. Suddenly it brought with it a blinding swirl of snow, and in seconds the full force of a blizzard was upon them. Morgan bent into it, nearly double, but she could make no headway. She could see nothing, not Toivo in front of her, not even her own feet.

Toivo placed a rope in her hands. "This could last for hours," he shouted in her ear. "We'll have to make a shelter."

Morgan tied the rope to her waist and followed Toivo. With their backs to the storm, they tramped out a rectangle roughly eight feet by four feet. Toivo thrust a shovel at Morgan. She was to dig out the area while he cut ice blocks from a quarry he had marked off at one end.

As she worked, Morgan tried to shut herself off from the chaos that roared around her. They had tramped a foot-deep depression, and she doubled it before her shovel hit the solidity of the old ice. Toivo came with his axe and helped her excavate another foot, but the blizzard blew in new snow almost faster than they could dig.

Toivo heaved out a last shovelful of snow and ice. "It'll have to do," he shouted. "Let's get the roof on." He and

Morgan dragged the square blocks from the quarry and positioned them in an A-frame over the excavation, packing the joinings with snow that quickly froze to a tight seal. Inside they shoveled out the blizzard snow and spread a ground sheet. Toivo secured the entrance and cleared the vent tubes, and they were safely cocooned.

Nothing from outside reached them, no wind and no sound. They could not stand, but there was room to move and to stretch limbs. A milky light filtered through the roof ice, alternately translucent and opaque, as the snow outside piled up and was blown away by the wind.

Morgan's mind thawed with her body. The delay . . . Arnie and Vulpius . . . She spoke her thoughts. "They'll be holed up, too, won't they?"

Toivo nodded. "No way anyone can travel in this. There's nothing to do but wait it out."

They arranged their packs in one end of the narrow burrow. Toivo unfolded the stove while Morgan found the food pouches. Soon they were eating pemmican stew and drinking bitter grubber tea.

"Sinop," Toivo said. "It's a stringy root that grows under the snow. You find it in spots where Argus gives the most color. Remarkable vitamins." He smiled over the rim of his cup, his weathered skin crinkling into two fans of wrinkles. "Drink up. It'll keep you young."

Toivo's white hair and fringe of whiskers framed a face that was both ancient and ageless. In the glow from the stove it resembled carved wood, all juttings and hollows. His eyes were hooded, but Morgan was still conscious of their power.

She risked a personal question. "How young has it kept you?"

He grinned again. "Ninety. I don't account it much. Some of our old ones are coasting past a hundred and still out every day on skis."

"You attribute it to this?" She swished the murky liquid.

"No, I was joking. Grubbers have always been long-lived; it's another Argus effect. Those of us who've made the journey can expect more years than you'd ever believe."

Morgan took a sip of the tea. What else besides vitamins did it contain? she wondered. But she swallowed it all the same. Sitting comfortably with a young-old psychic in a cylinder of ice beneath a raging storm, she wasn't inclined to be either skeptical or suspicious. "When did you make your journey?" she asked. "Was it before you met Ahlwen?"

"I'd never heard of him then," Toivo said. "I was a young pup on fire for a girl in our camp. She ran off with some one else, and I thought what life there was left for me wasn't worth preserving. I took off for the glacier, thinking she'd be sorry when she heard. Mostly no one came back from up there, and if they did, they could do . . . strange things. Maybe, I thought, if it happened to me, I could even make her love me."

"Had you any special gifts before then?"

"If I did, I didn't know it. Like I said, I was raw — barely been on my first hunt and mush-headed as they come.

"There's a place in the middle of this ice sheet where the air is still and it hardly ever snows. The light is . . . like looking into the eye of God. I don't know how I ever made it there. Just luck, I guess. That's where I met Anders. I was in bad shape: starved, half blind, both feet frozen. But I'd seen the colors where they come together, and I didn't know where I was, or who, or anything except what was happening inside me.

"Anders found me. He was living there then, all alone, in an icehouse about the size of this one. He was just back from Astra and working on what he'd learned there. Letting Argus work on it. He saved my feet and my mind, and when I went back to my camp I had the inner sight and I was a healer."

"Did you get the girl?"

"No, she wouldn't have anything to do with me. I lived off by myself, and most folks were scared of me. I didn't fit in anymore, and when I heard about Anders starting his own camp, I took off without a goodbye to anyone and joined him."

"How long ago was this?"

"Oh, sixty, seventy years."

"Then Ahlwen must be . . . at least your age." Morgan thought of the sleek, smooth-faced man she had met and could scarcely credit it.

A twitch appeared at a corner of Toivo's mouth. "There's a lot about him that'd surprise you. He's worlds beyond the rest of us in every way, and he's still growing, learning. You've got no cause to be worried about your daughter. All of us at his camps, we count ourselves lucky just to be near him."

Dee, Morgan remembered, had said much the same thing.

"This 'mission' Dee mentioned in her letter — what is it? Arnie thinks she'll be selling flowers in the streets for Ahlwen."

The twitch returned. "That's the last thing he'd ever encourage, though I've no doubt there'll be strange goings-on in his name someday that he's never even dreamed of.

"No, the mission is to build on what we have here in Lumisland. What Argus has given us. To preserve it. If all of Jaspre knew what we do, this talk of a second Argus would die out fast. I don't put much stock in it myself, but you've come from Friishaven — what do you think? Is there any real danger?"

His naiveté surprised Morgan. "You ought to be more concerned," she said. "With SEF pushing the Argus Two plan, it's almost certain to be adopted. And the SEF officers are the ones you have to convince, not the people of Jaspre."

"Then perhaps you would help us."

"Ha! I'd be your worst possible spokesperson. And what makes you think I'd even want to try after what you've done to Dee?" She held up her hand before Toivo could protest. "No, I don't think, like Arnie, that you're holding her against her will. But there are different forms of persuasion." She didn't say it, but after all that had happened, Morgan wasn't even sure that she would want to preserve Lumisland. If Ahlwen lost his source of power, he would no longer have a following. Dee would almost certainly return to her family, and Arnie would have no need for revenge.

She wished it would happen now! That Argus would be disarmed, the glacier melted, and her family restored.

Instead, her true situation came back to her in chilling clarity. She imagined Arnie sitting out the storm in another ice burrow, consumed by his deadly intent.

"He won't wait long," she said. "He'll brave the blizzard to get to Ahlwen." Her cramped muscles quivered. "What do you suppose it's like outside now? Hadn't we better check instead of sitting in here blind?"

Toivo didn't move. "No use. It's too late to travel now."

He was right. Except for the burning fuel capsule that lit up the stove, it was dark inside the icehouse. Outside was freezing death.

Their sleeping bags, when they spread them out, filled the floor space. Morgan removed her boots and parka and crawled gratefully into the insulated softness.

In the morning, Toivo dug his way to the surface and reported that the blizzard still raged. They remained holed up all that day, with Morgan increasingly frantic at losing so much time.

Toivo bore the delay with greater patience, spending hours in trancelike meditation. They had pemmican for only one more meal, and a few food cubes, but he had told her not to be concerned. He ate little, probably able, she guessed, to regulate his body's metabolism.

Perhaps he could teach her to do the same.

He stirred, and focused his eyes. "We can try, if you wish to learn," he said.

His sensitivity to her thoughts no longer surprised her. "Why not? We have the time," she said.

They sat facing one another, with fingers lightly touching. "Your mind is more powerful than you realize," Toivo said.

"If you channel your thoughts properly, you can control processes that you usually think of as involuntary. The organs, glands, nerves. Even to the cellular level."

He increased the pressure of his fingers. "Visualize your circulatory system. Your heart, veins, arteries. Can you do it?"

Morgan formed an extended mental image. She nodded.

"Now *feel* it. Feel the blood flowing smoothly in, the pumping, the release."

She tried but could not get beyond her concentration.

"Let me help you." He looked into her eyes, drawing her into his own consciousness.

She gasped as her image came to life. *Her* life, flowing, pulsating.

"Your hand," he said. "Each capillary."

She felt it, the spidery network that reached to the tips of her fingers.

"Your foot."

It worked again.

"Try it now, the same thing." He averted his eyes, but left her the touch of his fingers.

She succeeded with intense effort.

He withdrew his fingers. "Now by yourself."

She struggled until sweat beaded her face.

"Not so hard," he said. "You're too tense. Clear your mind now, and we'll try again later."

Toivo prepared half of the remaining food. Morgan allowed him to convince her mind that she wasn't hungry, and she ate as sparingly as he. They napped, then continued the instruction until dark.

13

The storm blew itself out during the night. In the morning, Morgan and Toivo dug themselves to the surface through a great drift that had built up around the projecting roof of the icehouse. The new snow was easy to shovel away. Outside, it lay over the ice like a smooth, glittering carpet, the mound of their campsite the only protrusion for what looked like hundreds of miles in all directions. Argus, a liquid, blood-red half globe surrounded by a series of intersecting arcs, was visible through a hazy white veil.

As Morgan watched, the veil dissolved. She turned from the spectacle, uneasy even with the protection of her goggles.

She found no escape. To the north, beyond the deepening snow colors, an immense sheet of exposed ice glowed, brilliant as Argus itself. There was no horizon; the ice reflected into the sky, going on forever.

Toivo took new bearings. "With this weather, we'll make Varma easily by nightfall," he said. They strapped on their packs and bade goodbye to the icehouse. The people at Varma would use it later as a food cache, Toivo said as he marked the location on his chart.

The snow deposited by the blizzard had formed a good surface for skiing. Argus colors blended one into another as Morgan followed Toivo. The only sound was their breathing and the scrape of their skis in the snow. Ahead, the fiery sheet continued to rise into the sky, coming no nearer though they covered mile after mile at a pace Morgan would never have dreamed possible.

Two hours sped by. Argus was a complete sphere, with only one faint companion arc behind it. Morgan exchanged her face mask for a layer of protective grease and breathed more comfortably. She scarcely felt her pack, even after three and then four hours.

They ate a standing lunch of thermos tea and body-warmed food cubes, the last of their rations. Toivo said he knew of a nearby cache, but Morgan voted to go straight on. Argus continued to favor them, and when the ice was flat they sped across it as though they were on an enormous rink. Even when they came to a patch of low, wind-waved ice, they scarcely slowed, Morgan leaping ridges almost as smoothly as Toivo.

The colors continued ever more dazzling. *You feel like you could do anything,* Karla had once said of the Argus effect. Morgan didn't wonder that Dee had been seduced. To find such strength after she had been so ill. A clear purpose after being so confused. If only Arnie could see it. Morgan recanted her thoughts of the previous evening, about wanting Argus disarmed.

Toivo wore no protection on his face. He even removed his goggles for short periods, and when he did so, he appeared transported. Morgan felt curiously lightheaded herself. She was somehow separated from her body, yet she was also more aware of it than she had ever been, in perfect control, it seemed to her, of every physical process.

The shimmering mirage continued on the horizon, tantalizing with its apparent nearness.

Morgan skied, floating, to Toivo. "How far is it?" she asked, pointing.

Toivo's lips scarcely moved, but his voice came to her clearly. "Farther than it looks. A week's trek, at least, from Varma. But it doesn't need to be the ordeal that it is for some, that it was for me. Not if your mind is attuned and you know the ways of the ice."

Morgan thought of Dee again, and of Britt. To open one's mind to its limits . . . She almost envied them.

They continued into the north, the colors deepening as Argus sank slowly behind them. The ice surface was flat with no discernible landmarks, but Toivo slowed and waved Morgan to his side. "We're getting close to Varma," he said. "Another hour. Stay near me from now on.

"The *elukka miehet*," he explained. "Crazies, you've heard them called. They have their tunnels and caves around here."

"They'd attack us?"

"Only you."

"You said they're like guards protecting the camp?"

"In a way, but not by any design of ours. They recognize the Argus power in Anders and in those of us who are adepts, and they won't touch us. Anyone else is in certain danger. The dwellers at Varma put out food for them, but it's never enough. They're always half starved."

Morgan moved even closer to Toivo. The icescape around them appeared peaceful and undisturbed, but she peopled it with monstrous phantoms. Toivo pointed to a slight protuberance off to their left, a mound glinting with Argus gold. "That's one of their burrows. I'd just as soon not test my powers protecting you. Let's get away fast."

Toivo took off like a windstorm, and Morgan strained to stay with him. She sensed that he was holding himself back for her, and she called up greater strength. Her heart thudded until she steadied it with effort, but when she sighted a tiny, dark figure coming directly toward them, all her control fled.

Toivo slowed. "It's an *elukka*," he said. "A wounded one." He narrowed his eyes. "A lasgun wound. Arnie's gotten here first."

Despair numbed Morgan until reason and a degree of hope returned. "But then . . . if he shot the *elukka,* it means he's all right."

"Maybe. An *elukka* wouldn't ordinarily run, though. Even wounded, it would stay and fight. I don't know what it means. Someone from the camp must have intervened and sent it away." He frowned, but gave Morgan a gesture of reassurance. "It's too weak to be dangerous. You'll be all right. Let's see what we can find out."

The creature drew nearer, lurching as it approached. Toivo tensed himself, and it halted.

Gaunt, hairy, with blackened skin and a skeletal, nightmarish face, it bore little resemblance to a human. Its right arm hung stiff and useless, and dark, frozen blood stained the torn hirvisen hide that wrapped its torso and legs.

It growled, deep in its throat. Its left hand clutched a grubber hunting knife, which it waved in ineffectual swipes. Swaying, it collapsed to its knees and then to a twitching heap on the snow.

Toivo placed his hand on the creature's head and closed his eyes. His face tightened.

He removed the hand. "There's nothing I can read," he said. "There never is."

"Do we just leave it here?"

He touched it again. "It's dead now. It will be eaten."

Morgan shuddered. Toivo mumbled words over the body and threw some more snow. "There'll be others here soon," he said. "We can't linger."

They took off at their former pace, Toivo turning his head frequently to scan in all directions. They traveled a half hour without incident before he pointed in the distance to something that Morgan could not see at first.

She blinked and narrowed her eyes to make out a dark blotch on the colored surface of the snow. As she continued to stare, it separated into individual black specks, then into an image so clear that she might have been looking through a scope: *elukka miehet* at a grisly feast.

One of the creatures turned, and Morgan saw that it held the bloody remains of a human leg.

She blocked out the vision, unwilling to see more.

If Toivo had watched the rest, he said nothing. He turned with a spray of snow, jamming his poles hard into the surface. Morgan too pushed off with all her strength. She bent into a racer's crouch, pumping her legs as fast as they would go.

Toivo swerved again, back to their former direction. Now Morgan could see a change in the colors before her, a deeper shade that signified a rise in the terrain.

Toivo waved, encouraging her. "Varma," he shouted.

They crossed an expanse of wave ice, and Morgan saw a long, low hill glowing in hues of purple. Closer, she could define a series of mounds, some of them issuing puffs of smoke or steam.

Toivo slowed his pace.

Morgan's face was stiff under the layer of grease, and her legs threatened to collapse. She coasted to a stop. The scene she had glimpsed was still with her, and all she could think of was what she might find in Varma. Which one — Arnie or Vulpius — had the beast men devoured?

Toivo shouted and waved for her to come. She couldn't move until she took off her goggles and received the full strength of Argus's restoring energy.

Her legs worked again, enough to take her to where Toivo waited at an underground entrance. They removed their skis and descended precisely cut ice stairs to what looked like a storage room, then more stairs and a downward-sloping tunnel. Morgan heard voices, and figures came to meet them.

Toivo greeted friends, then more, until the narrow corridor was packed. They moved into a larger space, separated, and Morgan searched vainly.

Vulpius came into the room, and her heart seemed to freeze in her breast.

She was on her back, with faces swimming before her

and voices coming from a distance. She breathed a whiff of something pungent, and her vision cleared.

Vulpius's head and both arms were bandaged. He bent over her with a deep frown of concern. "He's alive," he said. "Arnie's alive."

Morgan sat up. "Where is he? Can I see him?"

"He's here. *Jo,* I'll take you to him. He's hurt bad, but maybe seeing you will help.

"But how did you get here? And why?" he asked as he helped her to her feet.

"With Toivo," Morgan said. "To stop . . . whatever it was that happened. Only we got caught by the storm. You did, too, didn't you? But who . . . what was it those *elukkas* were eating? I saw them."

"It was one of their own that Arnie shot. It *could* have been us. God, I'd heard, but I never believed —"

"This way." It was Toivo. "Anders is with him, but I'm told he may not be able to save him."

"He must!" Morgan seized Toivo's arm. "What about you, the things you can do —"

"Let's wait and see," Toivo said. They hurried through the soft light of another tunnel made of smooth ice walls.

Anders Ahlwen met them at an open doorway. He led them into a small room to a bed where Arnie lay. "I've tried to heal him," he said, shaking his head. "But he won't allow it."

Arnie's face was waxen. A pinkish froth issued from between his lips, and his breath was a labored gurgle. The bandages that wrapped his chest and belly were soaked with blood.

14

"I can't do anything," Ahlwen said. "He's using his energy to fight me, and it's making him weaker."

Morgan knelt by the bed. She removed her layers of gloves and rubbed Arnie's cold hand between her two. "I'm here," she whispered. "It's me, Morgan."

There was no response, and she raised her voice, fighting to keep it steady. "I've come to help you, Arnie. I love you. You have to live, for me and for Dee and Matt and Danny. We need you. Please, for all of us."

Arnie opened his eyes. "Morgan?" His hand moved in hers, his fingers pressing feebly. "Don't . . . don't let them mess with me."

The effort brought a coughing spell and more blood. "Do something!" Morgan implored, turning to the others. "What kind of healers are you?"

Ahlwen moved to the bed. "I've stitched the external wounds, but he was clawed deeply. Nearly disemboweled.

The *elukka* had gotten hold of a knife and cut right through his clothing. I could repair the internal damage if he'd only let me, but I can't do anything without his cooperation."

"Get me a doctor," Arnie whispered. "A real doctor."

"We're on the glacier," Morgan said. "Satama's five days away. I know what Ahlwen can do. Please let him try."

Arnie's words came faintly. "No. Keep him away." His eyes closed and his hand loosened. The labored, liquid breathing resumed.

Ahlwen checked the bandages and placed a blanket over Arnie. "I've suctioned his lungs, but it does no real good. He'll die soon if I can't get inside him."

"What about physical surgery?" Morgan asked. "He might not object to that. Could you do it?"

"I'm not trained, and we haven't the facilities. We've never had the need for them." Ahlwen sighed. "I know we could save him, Toivo and I together. If we could both focus —"

"How is he?" asked a frightened voice from the doorway.

Dee came into the room, a pale figure in furs, with red, swollen eyes. "Has he changed his mind? If only he'd listen —" She caught sight of Morgan. "You came! I'd hoped — but how did you know?"

They embraced. Dee felt strong and solid through the bulky clothing. Her cheeks appeared fuller, too, and aside from the strain in her face, she looked extraordinarily well.

"I started out after Arnie," Morgan said.

"Thank God you're here!" Dee gripped both of Morgan's arms. "You can do it; you can persuade him. I've tried, but he won't listen to me. He thinks I've been . . . subverted. He's afraid that we're all evil here, that we'll try to twist his mind and change him. You've got to convince him to trust Anders." The grip tightened, almost painfully. "If he dies, I couldn't bear it! It would be my fault!"

Morgan pried loose Dee's fingers and backed away. Then she put her hands to her face.

"You've got to!" Dee repeated.

Arnie's voice echoed: *Don't let them.*

She had to think, but there was no place, no time. She felt Toivo's hand on her shoulder. "You can lead him," he said. "You have the strength and the ability. You can enter his mind through what you two have shared. Through your love. He'll accept you, and through you, us."

"And then deliver him to Ahlwen?" It was Vulpius's bitter voice.

Toivo answered. "To be healed."

"No, to be captured," Vulpius said.

Morgan turned from them both. Who was she, to make such a decision? She couldn't see into the future, couldn't read Ahlwen's motives. There was no misreading Arnie, but to obey him would be to let him die.

A gurgling cough came from the bed. "We haven't much time," Ahlwen said.

Morgan stopped agonizing. She might be wrong — some would say so, she knew — but it seemed to her that she had only one choice. She would betray Arnie's trust if she had to, to save his life.

"I'll try," she said to Toivo. "What do I do?"

"The same as when I focused on you in the icehouse. The way I helped you to regulate your metabolism. You can do it for Arnie. Begin with a memory that he'll want to share. Something that will bind him to you. Once you establish contact, he should follow you with little effort on your part."

Morgan tried to quell a fluttering in her stomach. She felt overly warm and removed her parka.

Dee offered a cup of lukewarm sinop tea. She tried to drink, but her throat was too tight. What if I fail? she thought. And what if I don't, and he hates me for it? "I'm afraid," she said.

Dee put her hands over Morgan's. "You mustn't be. I've had it done to me. Anders cured my deafness. You only have to trust him. He takes you inside your body, and you let him work miracles."

The word disturbed Morgan. "There are no miracles," she said. "Not even from Ahlwen. Your deafness could have been psychological. Arnie's injuries certainly aren't. I'm not at all sure that Ahlwen can save him, but" — her voice wobbled — "I don't know what else to do!"

She hurried to the bed before her will could falter.

Vulpius left with a muttered curse. Dee brought a stool, and Morgan sank down on it gratefully. Ahlwen and Toivo sat on opposite sides of the bed, Toivo next to Morgan. Dee left at Ahlwen's motion, dropping the curtain after her.

Morgan took Arnie's hand. "Speak to him," Toivo whispered. "Get him to look at you and to share what you're thinking."

She took him back to New Terra. "The farm," she said. "Remember how hard we worked? That soypod harvest in all the rain?"

Arnie moved his lips, his eyes focused on Morgan. "All that rain." The words came with halting effort. "Didn't think we'd . . ."

Morgan touched his lips, holding his concentration and guiding him to continue subvocally.

". . . *make it. Sure, I remember.*"

They remembered together.

Arnie came in from the fields, his boots caked with black clayey mud. His shirt clung damply to his broad shoulders, and droplets of water glistened in his hair and beard.

Morgan joined him on the porch. "Why didn't you come in sooner?" she said. "I ran when that downpour started."

"I knew it wouldn't last." They both looked toward the lake, over the green fields that had drunk thirstily and that now steamed in the slanting rays of Epsilon Eridani. "That soypod is ready to pull, rain or shine," Arnie said. "I'll bet on more rain, though, and that means we can't use the harvester. Ground's too gummy."

"I'd better get Dee and Danny from Valdisport," Morgan said. "They can miss a few days of school."

"I'll help, too." Matt crawled out from his private kingdom in the space under the porch. "I can pull soypods, can't I, Daddy?"

Arnie rumpled Matt's hair. "Sure, son, I can use all the hands I can get."

It would be their best crop yet, Morgan thought. And how Arnie deserved it after all the bad years. After failures that had defeated so many of their neighbors.

Arnie reached for Morgan, and she moved into his damp embrace. "You deserve it," he said with a smile.

The Arnie on the bed remained with Morgan when she

returned them to the present. *The house is waiting,* she reminded him. *That covered terrace that we never finished, where we were going to sit for hours someday in our airfloat rockers, looking at the view. Our land all the way to the lake.*

She could feel him still with her, wanting their future as much as she. She spoke to his will to live. *It's up to you, totally. You will be repairing your own body. The healers will only direct you, give you their energies.* She squeezed his hand. *I'll be with you, too.*

He was still open, and she nodded to Ahlwen and Toivo. They bent over him and moved their spread hands lightly over his torso, barely touching the bandages. Morgan maintained her eye link until Ahlwen gradually replaced her, insinuating himself so gently that Arnie offered no resistance.

Morgan continued to hold Arnie's hand, but otherwise she was a spectator. The two healers worked in silence, concentrating intently. At times Morgan could see a pulsing aura around both of them, and she could not look at their eyes.

An hour passed, and another. Arnie twitched occasionally, and once or twice he mumbled thick-tongued words that Morgan could not understand. She watched his color, and it improved markedly as the healing continued. His pulse was steady, and at the end of the second hour he was breathing without the frightening gurgle.

Change the bandages, someone directed Morgan. She found clean ones on the table by the bed, as well as nulbac powder and sponges and hot water.

The long, jagged wounds that covered Arnie's chest and belly had been neatly stitched, but they were seeping blood. Morgan sponged, sprinkled powder, and taped on fresh pads.

Ahlwen and Toivo both sat slumped in attitudes of extreme weariness. Ahlwen lifted a drained face. "Could you . . . some of that tea?"

Morgan served it. "Did it go as you'd hoped?" she asked. Arnie appeared to be sleeping peacefully, but she had no idea of his true condition.

"He'll recover," Ahlwen said. "It will take time, but he'll heal now on his own. All he needs is rest and the right kind of food. Which we can see that he receives."

"I'll stay with him," Morgan said. "You and Toivo look as though you need rest yourselves. I . . . we owe you so much."

"You owe us nothing," Ahlwen said. "The healing is a gift from Argus. Perhaps later we can talk about how we can best preserve it." He rose stiffly. Both he and Toivo moved to the door with the gait of old men.

They left the room, and in a moment Dee and another woman came in.

Dee was smiling before she even looked at Arnie. "What did I tell you?" she said. She hugged Morgan and touched Arnie lightly on the face. "He'll sleep now for hours. Why not get some rest? Ilmi and I will watch him."

Morgan recognized the woman from Ahlwen's First Station camp. She had made a fast trip, Morgan thought, but her mind was getting too fuzzy to puzzle out whys or hows.

"I'll show you where you can sleep," Dee said, helping Morgan up.

It was late evening, Morgan realized. Outside, it would be dark. Though her thoughts were foggy, she remembered to check Arnie again. The bleeding had stopped, and his breathing was still regular. She let herself be led away.

15

Morgan awakened in a narrow room lined with rows of cots. Dim ice light filtered through translucent patches of the ceiling, indicating that she had slept long.

Too long! She dressed hurriedly, found a surprisingly civilized bathroom next door, and set out to check on Arnie.

The curtain of his room was down, but Morgan heard voices inside. Familiar, normal voices. She released a tightly held breath.

Arnie was sitting propped up, eating from a steaming bowl while Dee hovered over him. "One more. I know you can do it," she urged.

He saw Morgan and pushed the bowl aside. "That's all; I'll finish it later."

"It'll get cold," Dee said.

"I'll see that he eats," Morgan said. "I'll take over now."

Dee handed the bowl to Morgan. "It's important. The tea, too. Then he should rest again. He shouldn't get too tired."

Arnie's color was good. He wore a tie-front tunic with a

light fur over his shoulders. He was washed and shaved, even his hair trimmed.

"Ilmi did it," Dee said. "She left just now to go to bed, but she's been fussing over him all morning. She feels responsible, because Arnie and Vulpius got here by following her."

"She and some others were coming to warn Ahlwen about me," Arnie said. "They left good tracks."

"And you," Morgan said to Dee, "have you been here all night, too?"

"I slept some in the chair."

"Then go now and get some rest yourself."

"I will." Still, she lingered by the bed.

Morgan turned to Arnie. "You're really feeling well? Any pain? How are those wounds?" She opened the tunic; the dressings were fresh and white.

Arnie spread his hands. "I'm fine. Believe it. Nothing hurts as long as I don't move too much. I can get up tomorrow if I'm a good boy and eat all this pap. Do me a favor — finish it for me."

Morgan stirred the gruel and tasted a spoonful. "It's not so bad." She imitated Dee's maternal tone. "Now, one for you."

They finished it together.

Morgan poured the tea. "Sinop," she said. "I'm told it has properties from Argus."

Arnie looked away. "So, it appears, do people."

There was an awkward silence. "You understand it now, though, Daddy," Dee said softly. "You know why I want to stay."

Arnie suddenly looked tired. "We'll talk about it later," he said.

Dee walked slowly to the door, with backward glances.

"She wants your approval," Morgan said when they were alone. "Or at least your understanding."

"I know." Arnie sighed. "I have a lot of thinking to do. That healing . . . I . . . I'm in debt to Ahlwen, like it or not. To you, too." He avoided her eyes. "It seems I was a prize fool."

Knowing how he must feel, she squirmed for him. "You were never that, Arnie," she said. "You had a lot of pressures, and you let your emotions take over. Anyway, you'll be fine now, and we can go back to Friisland together. Nurmi can accept it or not. This exile of mine has lasted long enough!"

Arnie didn't answer. He was thinking about Dee, Morgan guessed.

She tried to bring him back. "Matt's staying with Jazmin," she said with forced brightness. "She'll keep him entertained — you know her — but he'll be wild when we get home with you safe. He was so worried."

"He'll be glad to see you, anyway."

Again Morgan felt his shame. But he would get over it. "When we're away from the snow, we can forget all this," she said.

"How can we, with Dee still here?"

Morgan busied herself with the boiling teapot. "Do you want more?" she asked.

He shook his head.

"Then you're supposed to rest." She removed his bolster

and helped him to lie flat. "Are you warm enough?" She pulled up his comforter.

"Yes," he said. He closed his eyes, shutting her out. His mind needed healing, too, she thought. But he would have to do it himself.

She watched over him while he slept. After an hour, the door curtain parted and Dee came in.

"I thought you went to bed," Morgan said.

Dee was snow-dusted and glowing. "I couldn't waste the time. Not when it's so glorious outside!"

Morgan led her away from the bed. "We mustn't disturb him."

Dee lowered her voice, but her energy still vibrated. "It's snowing jewels. No wind, just rubies and emeralds drifting down. You've got to go up and see!"

Morgan wasn't tempted. Not here, with Arnie. "No," she said, "I've had enough of that for a while. And what about those *elukkas*?"

Dee made a disparaging motion. "Oh, I have to have someone with me. You will, too, until they get to know our scent." She took off her parka and shook it. "You should go out soon, though. Anders and Toivo have already been, and everyone says they're fully restored."

Morgan wasn't swayed. "I don't doubt it. But I'm fine as I am." She studied Dee, who appeared almost miraculously changed from the listless wraith she had been in Friisland. Her cheeks were pink and her eyes sparkled with vitality.

Was she changed in less visible ways as well? "I can tell that the snows agree with you, but what about other Argus benefits? Have you felt them?"

189

Dee clasped her hands. "It's like I'm on the brink of the most exciting adventure. Anders says I have tremendous potential. I have a few blocks to overcome — maybe my old injury — but he's given me exercises to do, and every time I'm out on the snow I feel myself opening up more."

Morgan looked toward the bed. "He — well, both of us, actually — we're not happy about leaving you here."

"Then stay! Anyone who wants to is welcome."

"Arnie, too?"

Dee giggled.

"Not very likely," Morgan agreed. "No, it's not for us, but you — you'll come home again, won't you, after a while? With your new strengths, you'll be able to pick and choose a career."

Dee backed up a step. "I'm surprised at you, Morgan! What did you think? That this is some kind of a tourist camp where I can come and go? I thought you understood. *This* is my career. I have a *purpose* to my life now."

She should have known, Morgan thought. She *had* known, but she also had to make the attempt. Now, she tried to recoup. "Yes, it's very impressive, this whole complex. I haven't seen too much, but —"

"I'll take you around." Dee flashed a forgiving smile. "Let me get someone to stay with Dad. I'll be right back." She was gone before Morgan could object.

Arnie had not stirred. Morgan was glad he hadn't heard. Perhaps gratitude to Ahlwen would soften him, she thought. Perhaps it would lead him to look more leniently on Dee's new allegiance.

At least one could always hope.

Dee returned with a young man and hurried Morgan out. "There's so much to show you," she said. "You saw one of the sleeping rooms. There's another big one like that and half a dozen small ones. The room where we do all the cooking is down here, and I know you'll want to see the power plant."

"If you don't mind, could I have a bath first?" Morgan begged. "I saw a tub, and I'm so filthy."

"Of course!" Dee pulled Morgan along to the washroom.

"Wait a few minutes," she said, moving a gauge on a squat, standing honeycomb of lurite coils.

They began to glow. "What's the power source?" Morgan asked. "Wait. Don't tell me. It's Argus, isn't it?"

Dee beamed. "It's brand new. They've just got the cells to working."

"Those globes, too?"

Dee nodded. "It's made a big difference to Varma. Before, they used fuel capsules, and you know how expensive they are."

"Quite an accomplishment with everything having to be hauled in." Morgan eyed the water heater, wall panels, pipes, and basins.

"They've been working here longer than we've been alive," Dee said. "*Varmapaikka,* that's the real name of the camp. It means 'safe place,' and you can feel as easy here under the ice as you would in Friishaven."

"What about shifting?" Morgan asked. "If the glacier should move —"

"It doesn't. Not enough to measure. The temperature's constant all year, and they don't have earthquakes."

191

A valve hissed, and Dee tested the water. She let it run. "I'll get you a towel. Do you want clean underclothes?"

"If you have them."

"Sure. I'm in charge of the laundry this week."

Dee had always hated domestic work. Morgan marveled again at the change as she stripped and stepped into the tub. "This new 'purpose' you mentioned. I know it's not washing clothes."

"Be serious! You know what it is. You talked to Toivo."

"You mean preserving Argus power?"

"We have access to something wonderful here. Something that will enable us to grow beyond anything you can imagine. You should hear Anders talk when we're all gathered. About the other dimension and the life of the spirit. He's an inspiration to all of us. This" — she gestured around at the washroom equipment — "none of this is really important. Not to him. He goes out on the glacier for weeks and stays in a hole no bigger than our food caches. When he comes back, he's all spirit. All power."

"Why build a place like Varma, then, if external comforts aren't important?" Morgan hugged her knees while Dee soaped her back. "I got an inkling, on the ice coming here, of what you're saying. Of how euphoric you can feel. But as far as I'm concerned — mmm, scrub some more there. Higher." She closed her eyes. "Nothing out on the snow can be better than this."

"I know you don't mean that. But I guess you've got your reasons for resisting." Dee came around to the front of the tub and knelt, resting her arms on the rim. "I haven't talked to Daddy yet. Not really. I've been afraid."

Morgan patted her hand. "Why don't you go now. Be there when he wakes up."

"But I was going to show you —"

"It'll keep. Go. Talk to your father."

Morgan ignored a final pleading look. Dee and Arnie had to make their peace, and Arnie might never again be as receptive.

After Dee left, Morgan dressed at her leisure. She dried her hair under the heat globe and twisted it into a low knot.

Someone came in. "Morgan Farraday?"

Morgan spun around. It was a man, a snowburned grubber. "Couldn't you have shouted a warning?" she said. "A minute ago I was in the tub."

"I know. I waited." His leathery face was impassive. "If you're ready, Anders will see you now."

She started to ask if she had a choice, thought better of it, and nodded.

The man led Morgan up a level to a small room near the surface. He parted the curtain for her and left.

Argus light shone through the clear ice roof, painting the uncovered walls and illuminating the figure sitting lotus fashion on a floor hide. The room contained no furnishings except a pile of furs in one corner. It had no heat globe, and the cold penetrated Morgan's clothing.

Ahlwen pointed to the furs. "Take them, as many as you need."

Morgan swathed herself in ketsi and spread another to sit on. Still, she shivered.

"You depleted yourself yesterday," Ahlwen said. "You should go to the surface soon."

"So I've been told already." Morgan wrapped the furs more closely. "But all I care about now is getting Arnie out of here safely."

"I see."

Remembering what Toivo had said about Ahlwen's age, Morgan studied his face vainly for evidence. Squint lines fanned out from the corners of his eyes, but otherwise the tanned skin was as smooth as a child's.

"Arnie should be ready to travel in a week," Ahlwen said. "Once the healing starts, it progresses quickly. I can do another session with him, if he'll permit it, to hasten the process."

"We're both so grateful."

"I only ask that you not reveal the location of Varma. We have our enemies."

"I won't; I promise. Actually, I couldn't, anyway. I could never find my way here again."

"Would you talk to Vulpius, too? I tried to, but he's inexorably hostile. I don't want to deal with a band of angry grubbers. There's been enough violence."

Morgan thought of the bestial creatures who guarded the camp. "You're well protected here," she said. "Too well."

"Ah, yes." He sighed. "I wish there was something I could do to help those damaged ones."

"You can't cure them?"

"No, their minds are gone. Burned out. They never survive long, and I'm not sure if it's even a kindness to feed them. The best I can do is ensure that there won't be others, at least from my camps."

"How can you do that?"

"I see that none of my people go on the journey unless they are ready. Unfortunately, I have no control over grubbers from other camps. If they come back ruined, they tend to gather here at Varma. I do what I can for them."

"Is anyone on the journey now? Anyone from here?"

"Only one. Britt Halsemer."

Morgan started. "But she can't have been in Varma long. Not long enough to be prepared."

"It isn't really a question of time. A person has the potential or she doesn't. Britt has tremendous discipline. She was more than ready mentally and had only to learn the necessary survival skills. If you stay here another two weeks, you can help us celebrate her return."

He seemed to Morgan too confident. "How will she get past the *elukkas?*"

"They won't trouble her. Britt will be an adept and able to control them."

"Or she'll be an *elukka* herself."

Ahlwen smiled and shook his head. "You still don't believe me. I said no one goes without my sanction, and I don't give it lightly."

"What about Dee?" Morgan asked.

"I can't tell you yet if she will be making the journey. She has much to learn."

"But you think so?"

"Yes, in all probability she will become an adept. She has the promise, and seldom have I seen such enthusiasm." He looked at her closely, kindly. "Surely you can see that she is happy with us."

Morgan nodded. "So it appears."

"And your husband? Is he reconciled?"

"Dee's talking to him now. I hope he'll understand."

"She will not be lost to you. By freeing her, willingly, you will ensure that." He rose. "I thank you for coming, and perhaps we will talk again. I hope your stay here is pleasant. *Rauha.*"

Morgan found Arnie and Dee alone. Arnie was sitting up with his eyes closed while Dee read to him.

"The flesh is both a prison and an illusion. With the key of Argus, we can unchain ourselves and perceive the truth beyond our external forms. There need be no limits to our understanding, no boundaries to our spirit. When our minds are unlocked, we transcend our humanity into a higher reality."

Dee looked up, her eyes shining. "It's *him.* The way he is. It's why he could heal you, Daddy. No regular doctor could have done it." She saw Morgan and held out the reader. "These are his own words, one of his lectures."

Morgan crossed to Arnie's bedside. "You're getting educated, I see."

He opened his eyes and reached for her hand. "Where have you been?"

Dee gathered up her bookspools. "I'll leave these. Morgan, you should look at them, too."

"Must you go?" Morgan said. She tried to guess how the interview had gone, but Arnie gave no clue.

"Yes, I've missed my morning work shift." Dee kissed her father. "I'll be back."

Arnie gave her a hug, but his eyes were troubled. Morgan

waited until Dee was well out of earshot before she spoke. "Are you resolved to her staying here?"

Arnie sighed. "What can I say? I'm not happy about it, but at least I know that she'll be okay physically. Mentally, I'm not so sure."

"You still have doubts about Ahlwen?"

He scowled. "I can't say anything against him now without sounding ungrateful."

"It's just you and me!"

He played with her fingers. "Oh, I know that the man isn't the unscrupulous crackpot I thought at first. He has real psychic powers, and he's not vindictive. He could have let me die. But what he's harnessed is only a freak effect of Argus, like the colors. There's no need to make it into a religion. This spiritual mumbo jumbo that Dee's been spouting — I've heard it before. From fire walkers on Tethys and bubble divers on Sagit IV. Not to mention all the loony spacers I've seen high on firmax powder. Dee's of age, though. I don't suppose there's anything I can do."

"We won't lose touch with her," Morgan said. "The group here is becoming more politically aware, according to Toivo. They'll need help in fighting Argus Two. I wouldn't even be surprised to find Dee lobbying against it sometime soon, back in Friishaven."

"You'll see her, then."

"We both will."

Arnie shook his head. "I won't be returning with you to Friisland."

"But . . . why? What will you do?"

He shrugged and released her hand. "I'm not sure. I'll try

to find some kind of work in Satama, maybe even the cannery. I only know that I can't face going back to Friishaven. Not after the way I've acted." He rubbed his face. "There's so much I don't understand. I . . . I just need some time to get my head straight again."

"You're tired," Morgan said. "You're still weak. Here." She lowered his pillows. "You've probably been sitting up too long. I know you'll think differently in a week when you're completely well. I know it!"

16

Morgan was wrong. A week later, she boarded the plane in Satama alone.

Arnie remained at the lodge, in spite of everything she said to dissuade him. He was fully recovered from his wounds, having skied out from Varma on his own power with her and Vulpius. At Third Station there had been a message from Commander Nurmi for Morgan to return at once to Friishaven.

Watching the coast of Lumisland recede, Morgan wondered what she would find at the end of her flight. She once had said to Arnie that her job was a "lost cause," and now she hoped it wasn't true. She hadn't even had a chance to show that she really cared about the schools. Dee had her own life now, and Arnie wanted to be left alone. Morgan was once more determined to succeed in her post.

Nurmi's message had been cryptic. "Need grubber input Argus Two. Return soonest." The commander had never been one to consider seriously any viewpoint but his own, and the sudden switch was puzzling. Was it the sole reason for her recall? She was hardly a Lumisland expert after barely a month on the continent.

She would have her answers soon. To pass the time, she pulled out her reader and slipped in a bookspool. It was a present from Dee, excerpts from Ahlwen's most recent lectures.

"Mumbo jumbo," Arnie had called it. As Morgan read, she couldn't be sure. A lot of it was the standard mystic's description of a transcendent spiritual reality, but Ahlwen also offered the possibility of a fleshly realization, a truly psychic race that could exist simultaneously on both planes. Children born of Argus adepts would be gene-altered to preserve their gifts away from the snow and would in turn breed true.

So far it had not worked, but Ahlwen still spoke of it as an end to be pursued. He concluded with a description of his vision, presented in glowing terms. Prolonged lifespans, physical and mental abilities beyond imagination, freedom from disease. A spiritual life as rich as the physical.

The next step in human evolution? Morgan admitted the possibility. A truly superhuman race. Dee had said that she felt on the brink of "an exciting new adventure." She believed wholeheartedly in Ahlwen's dream, and Morgan found herself hoping that he could somehow bring it about.

She had a commission of sorts, from him. At least, she had promised Toivo her last week in Varma to do what she could to prevent another Argus from destroying what the first had created.

She read her helex again. If Nurmi truly wanted grubber opinion, she might be able to do something after all.

Morgan had much to think about, and the flight seemed shorter than she remembered. She was surprised when the intercom announced the approach to Friishaven.

She leaned forward to gaze down upon a neat band of beach followed by one of rocks, one of grass and one of trees, each geometrically precise. The gray strip of the runway appeared, and they set down smoothly.

Argus and the real sun were moving away from their midday meeting, still joined in eye-searing brightness. Beyond the tarmac deplaning area, a small crowd watched a workman in coveralls paint over red letters sprayed above the doorway of the main building.

"——o HOME," read the remainder of the message. Most of the jeering onlookers sported "No Argus Two" and "SEF Go Home" buttons. A security guard watched nervously.

Justin DiVoto, dressed in civilian clothes, met Morgan inside the terminal. "Thank God you're not in uniform," he said.

He hurried her through the building. "Can't we wait for my baggage?" Morgan asked.

"I'll have it sent," he said. "I want to get out of here before we're recognized." He led the way to an unmarked groundcar. "I couldn't get a private flitter, and you can't go anywhere anymore in the SEF ones without being harassed."

The parking lot was festooned with large JASPRE FOR JASPRIANS banners, and a band of protesters, their arms linked, sat blocking the exit lane.

Justin slowed and stopped. "Now what?" he muttered as a young woman knocked on the window.

He opened it.

"It's him — DiVoto — I knew it!" she shouted.

A large, overripe vegetable sailed through the window opening. Justin ducked, and Morgan received it squarely on the side of her head.

The protesters formed a gauntlet, but the rest of the tomatoes squished harmlessly against closed glass. Justin whipped the car through the exit turns, cursing loudly, while Morgan attempted to clean herself with a tissue.

Justin handed her a handkerchief. "Sorry about the greeting," he said. "Things have hotted up since you left."

"So I see. But rotten tomatoes? They must really hate us."

"A minority of agitators. Farmers and damfool kids."

They entered the city proper, and Morgan spotted more signs and pedestrians wearing buttons. "Preserve the Snow — Rally Tonight," read a prominent notice. Another stated, "Preserve the Coast."

"It looks like more than a minority," Morgan said.

Justin tightened his lips. "They want everyone to think so. SEF Central especially. And the bad news is, they've succeeded."

"I've a feeling all this has something to do with my being here." Morgan noticed the route they were taking. "Hey, aren't you driving me home first? I can't go to the office looking like this."

"You can clean up there. Commander Nurmi's waiting. There isn't much time to prepare you."

"For what?" She leaned back, expecting the worst.

"I'll brief you. But first, how's Dee? I thought she and Arnie would come back with you."

"No, they're both staying in Lumisland."

"For how long? I got the impression from Jazmin that there was a problem, but she's awfully close-mouthed about it."

Morgan didn't answer, and he went on: "Actually, it's just as well Dee isn't here right now." He slowed the car for a line of placard-waving marchers. "I'd hate to have her exposed to this sort of thing. It bothered her before she left, and it's twice as bad now."

"Oh, Dee could cope all right," Morgan said drily. "She's changed."

"How? What do you mean?"

"You first. My briefing. We've lots of time to talk about Dee."

"Yes. Well." He drummed his fingers on the steering rod, then cleared his throat. "It seems that Central Headquarters has gotten wind of the opposition here to Argus Two. Lord knows how. Not through our channels, certainly. But now they're questioning the reports we've sent, and an S.E., a special envoy, is on the way here from Earth. Nurmi has to convince him that these rabble-rousers don't represent responsible Jasprian opinion. He's arranged meetings with business leaders from both Friisland and the Grace Islands. They're solidly behind him and the Argus Two plan. But he needs someone he trusts to speak for Lumisland, which after all will be the most affected. Can you see us dragging in some illiterate grubbers to meet with a special envoy?"

"So he's dragging in me. Does he think I can be trusted?"

"You value your career, don't you?"

"Yes, but I'm not going to cave in to him the way I did before. I was hired to run the schools, not promote his pet projects."

Justin whistled. "I almost hate to deflate you. But before you go up against the boss, you'd better know that he has an evaluation sheet on his desk, and it has your name on it.

"It's from Space Corps Central. They heard about the flap over your appointment, and what Nurmi has to say about it can make or break you." He reached over to pat her shoulder. "So you're wrong. You *will* play ball with him, or you're out of the game. And I don't mean just back to Lumisland. This time it's out for good, as in 'bad performance rating.' "

Justin's moue of sympathy had in it a hint of satisfaction. Morgan choked back angry words. The lieutenant had his career so firmly fixed to the commander's that nothing she could possibly say would sway him.

She pretended defeat. "I suppose he has a statement prepared for me. About how everyone in Lumisland hates the eternal winter and can't wait to get the snow melted and start growing potatoes."

"Something like that. It can't be too far from the truth, certainly. I understand it's pretty grim up there."

"In some ways." A plan was beginning to take form in Morgan's mind.

Justin returned to business. "Nurmi will fill you in on the meeting with the envoy. We're expecting him this evening, so you can see why we're pressed." He sniffed and wrinkled his nose. "Though I think we can spare you time for a shower. God, what a stink!"

The pedway in front of the SEF building was lined with protesters, but guards cleared the garage entrance.

Morgan wished they hadn't. She would have liked to see Justin the successful target of another garbage barrage.

He stepped out of the car, clean and pressed and smelling like a mountain meadow. "Ten minutes," he said as they parted. "I'll tell the commander."

Morgan didn't hurry. She had a leisurely shower that included a shampoo, picked up fresh fatigues from supply, and stopped in her office to see Jazmin.

"Matt's fine," Jazmin said after the squeals and hugs. "He's going to your house after school, to get it dusted and set up with flowers and all. So don't get there before he's ready."

"No danger. I've a meeting with the commander. Fill me in quickly. Nurmi's really in trouble over Argus Two?"

"Up to his neck. He pushed too hard, and now — you saw the reaction. The agitators for Jasprian independence latched on to his mistakes, and it looks as if SEF might lose control of the planet. Nurmi's desperate, with this Earth bigwig coming. If he can't convince the envoy that the Jasprians who matter really do want his plan, he may find himself off Jaspre as fast as he can pack. In charge of the Sirian sulfur pits."

"Just how strong is this independence movement?"

"It's hard to tell. They make a lot of noise, but the people I've talked to seem satisfied to let SEF run things, as long as we don't try to push Argus Two down their throats. They're very nervous about it."

"Hmm. So I thought." Morgan's confidence grew. "Thanks, Jazmin, for keeping Matt and all. It was a lot to ask."

"I was glad to help. I'll come over tonight with his things, if that's all right."

"Have dinner with us, if I have a chance to go shopping. Otherwise, we can all go out."

Morgan proceeded to her appointment, half an hour late. Justin was livid. "Where have you been? The commander canceled two appointments for you, and he's in there pacing the floor —"

"I'm sure he has work to occupy him." Morgan smiled sweetly and did a slow pirouette. "Do I pass inspection?"

"You look fine," Justin growled. "Come on." He opened the inner door. "Morgan Farraday, sir."

The commander studied her sourly. "Hmph! Lumisland seems to have agreed with you." He pointed to a chair. "Sit down. You too, Lieutenant."

Morgan sat facing the commander, with Justin a bit to the side.

"Lieutenant DiVoto says he briefed you on the situation here." He waited for her nod. "I'd like you to meet with the envoy, giving him your impressions of Lumisland. The harsh conditions, those people they call snowgrubbers. I understand they live barely above the level of animals. We have lots of holos. Here they are. You can look through the file later, and choose any that you feel are most representative. The scenes are all desolate; they should pretty well speak for themselves.

"Now, here are the projections for the same area, after Argus Two and the subsequent terraforming. It should be easy to imagine what the grubbers would think about it. You can speak for them with some authority, can't you?"

Morgan met his gaze directly. "Yes, I'll be glad to speak to the envoy," she said. "Will I be meeting him in my official capacity of Eastern Region school supervisor?"

"Yes, yes, of course," Nurmi said. "We'll tell the envoy that you've just returned from an extensive inspection tour of the north continent."

"And after I've had my little talk with him?"

"Why, you'll return to your office and your former duties. With an excellent letter from me to your Corps Personnel Bureau."

Morgan crossed her legs. "Ah, yes. That letter. An evaluation, actually, I understand. Would it be too much trouble for you to attend to it first, before I meet with the envoy? And I'd like to see both the original and the helex."

Justin sputtered, and the commander's face turned crimson.

"It's not that I don't trust you," Morgan said with a smile even more sugary than her first. "But these are trying times for all of us. Insecure times. I'm sure you'll understand my position."

"Too well," Justin said. "It's blackmail."

"That depends on where you're standing." She waited for Commander Nurmi to speak, and when he didn't, she rose to leave. "If it's to be a stalemate, I'm in no hurry. Contact me when you've decided — at my office or at home."

Nurmi stood up, too. A vein in his temple continued to throb. "Damn it, woman, I don't like to be pushed. Any other time you'd be out on your ear, but now — you'll have your letter. Report back here in two hours for final instructions, and there'd better not be any foul-ups."

"Yes, *sir*." Morgan turned to Justin, with a second small salute.

He glared back.

"See her out, DiVoto," the commander said.

In the outer office, Justin was coldly furious. "I hope you realize the position you've put *me* in. It was my idea to send for you. I did it mostly as a favor to Dee. The commander isn't going to thank me for the highhanded way you've behaved."

"I'm just looking out for myself," Morgan said. "There's no guarantee the envoy will buy what any of us have to say. If Nurmi loses, what kind of a rating do you think he'd give me? I have no intention of going down with him."

"It's your job — our job — to see that he doesn't lose." Justin's eyes had a look of desperation. "Perhaps you don't care what happens to me, but think of Dee. Her future lies with me, and for her sake you'll see that I don't go down, either."

"That's what you've been counting on, isn't it?"

"Are you implying that I'm using Dee? I thought you knew me better than that. I love Dee very much, and I'm sure she returns the feeling."

"Has she said so?"

"You know how shy she is. I haven't pressed her."

"You'll find Dee quite different now. You should talk to her again before you count on anything."

"I will, as soon as she returns. As soon as this Argus Two crisis is over."

Morgan felt a surge of sympathy for Justin that she hadn't expected. He was in for some unpleasant surprises. She couldn't tell him about Dee yet, though. Not until she had satisfied herself regarding Nurmi's letter and had met with the envoy. "You're right," she said. "Personal matters can wait. We both have important work to attend to. I should get to my office. Is there anything more, before I see the commander again?"

"Just don't antagonize him any further. He's in a tough spot, and his temper's thin."

"DiVoto!" came a roar from the deskcom.

Justin paled. "Good luck," Morgan mouthed as she hurried out.

In her own office, she looked through the file of holos Nurmi had given her. They were stills of unending snow, frozen oceans, and towering glaciers. All were in stark black and white, with no hint of the snow colors.

The envoy wouldn't accept that, she knew. He couldn't be so uninformed. Even she had heard of the colored snows long before coming to Jaspre.

She chose half a dozen scenes, mostly at random. She could handle the inevitable questions, not the way Nurmi would like, but neither could he accuse her of betrayal.

Jazmin came in with an armload of accumulated paperwork. "There's more in the computer," she said. "Shall I print it out?"

"Only what's urgent," Morgan said. "I'm seeing the commander again at three."

They settled down to work. Most of it was routine and easily dispatched, but Morgan initiated one change of personnel. "One teacher I know will be happy," she said as she reassigned Arin Molino to a Friishaven school.

Jazmin laid a sealed message tube on the desk. "This just came in from upstairs."

Morgan read Nurmi's letter with satisfaction. Her job was safe, at least from his blacklisting. About the Jasprians, though, she was still in doubt.

She looked up at Jazmin, who hovered curiously. "Go ahead, read it."

Jazmin did and raised a painted eyebrow. "Quite a turn-around."

"It's one victory," Morgan said. "But am I still a thorn in the side of the local press?"

"Oh, you can forget about that," Jazmin assured her. "There hasn't been a word for weeks. They've more important issues to get the public steamed up about."

"Good. All I want is the chance to prove myself."

Jazmin reminded her of the time, and they managed to clear the desk before Morgan reported upstairs again.

The commander's secretary presented her with the next day's schedule, a full printed sheet. It started with an informal breakfast reception for the envoy, followed by a forum on Argus Two with representatives from both SEF and Jaspre. Morgan was not included in the luncheon or the city tour, but later in the afternoon she had a half-hour private meeting with the guest of honor, sandwiched between a building contractor and a Grace Islands kelp farmer. In the evening she was to attend the formal banquet.

The listed Jasprian names meant nothing to Morgan, but she was sure they had all been carefully selected. Probably the tour route as well, cleared beforehand of anti-SEF displays. As thorough as Nurmi was, however, he couldn't disguise completely the true situation; she knew he was in for a rough time.

The door to his office was closed, and Morgan could hear loud male voices. "Do I have to wait?" she asked.

"No," the secretary said. "Everything is on the sheet. Just be on time. The schedule's tight."

Relieved, Morgan hurried out of the building before she could be recalled. She had time for shopping, after all, and loaded up on staples and Matt's favorite treats. She chose a fresh fish for dinner, with a kivit tart for dessert, and sparkling wine for her and Jazmin.

She juggled two bulging net bags on the bus, which fortunately was not crowded. Her SEF fatigues drew unfriendly stares, and she had a bad moment when a gang of youths wearing buttons boarded. When they spotted her, she got off quickly. She decided to walk the remainder of the way, and arrived at her house with aching arms.

Matt opened the door. "Mom!" He gasped in dismay. "You're too early!"

The door closed in Morgan's face. She heard frantic scurrying, and when it opened again, Matt was beaming. A WELCOME HOME banner hung lopsidedly across the hallway, and in the living room, ragged bunches of daisies in water glasses adorned every table.

Morgan dropped her bags and admired the display. "Hey, you didn't need to buy food," Matt said. "Dad left plenty. And I'm fixing dinner. You don't need to do a thing."

Morgan put away her purchases quickly. They would keep, even the fish. Matt shooed her out of the kitchen, and she tried to ignore the rattles and bangs and scrapes that issued through the door. Jazmin came, and the three ate a dinner of soup and sandwiches and chocolate-flavored drink. Dessert was more chocolate, in the form of lumpy, burned cookies.

Matt passed around the cookies a final time. "Now tell me about these new friends that Dee's staying with," he said. "Tell me about their city under the ice."

Morgan gasped. "Where did you hear about that?"

"Dad told me. When he called, before you came home. Oh, he said to tell you 'hi.'"

Morgan felt her face burn. Arnie knew her hours; he obviously hadn't wanted to talk to her.

Jazmin looked at her quickly, and then away. Matt bit his lip. "I'm sorry, I forgot to tell you," he said. "He was just explaining to me about why he was staying — his new job and all."

"What job?"

Matt's face registered confusion. "I thought you knew. He's taking Elsie's place, driving the crawler. He said he likes it fine."

Morgan tried to hide her embarrassment, but the evening ended on an awkward note. Jazmin left early, pleading things to do at home. Morgan and Matt cleaned up the kitchen together, and though Morgan did her best to appear cheerful, she knew that she wasn't fooling Matt. They talked a little, about Varma and about Matt's school, and they both went to their rooms as soon as it was dark.

17

The breakfast was held at the SEF cafeteria, which had been elegantly transformed with tablecloths and flowers. The envoy, to Morgan's pleased surprise, turned out to be a small, bright-eyed woman. "Call me Alia," she said to everyone, disdaining titles and formality. Commander Nurmi kept close to her side, discouraging any serious conversation, but Morgan received the impression in the few words they exchanged that the woman was completely unprejudiced, eager to meet as many Jasprians as she could and to hear all viewpoints.

Morgan had chosen a solitary table, where she sipped her juice and studied the scene for signs of the public temper. On the surface it could have been a purely social event, with the usual posing and light chatter. Yet there was an undercurrent of tension that proclaimed the high stakes, worried eyes that didn't match the smiles, and a nervous edge to the laughter.

Justin bustled through the crowd, tapping selected individuals to be presented to Alia. He was immaculately dressed in white silks, but his face was drawn. He saw Morgan and sent her a silent message of both warning and entreaty.

She did not respond. She pitied him, but he was young and well able to salvage his own career. Others, like the Lumisland grubbers, would not be as adaptable.

Alia stopped at Morgan's table. "I'm looking forward to this afternoon," she said. "I'm especially anxious to hear about the snows."

The commander wore a stiff smile. "Farraday is our expert on that," he said.

A group of Grace Islanders in bright robes claimed the envoy's attention, and the commander followed her to their table. Morgan wondered if the island resort owners were represented, and if Nurmi had reconciled them to their probable loss of property. Alia shook hands and asked questions, and Nurmi's face grew more and more rigid.

Morgan's thoughts turned to her coming interview. She would dispense with the black-and-white holos, she decided. She had color ones of her own that would better satisfy Alia, who she suspected was more than a match for Nurmi's scheming. Meeting the envoy had made Morgan feel less uneasy in her own role.

After the breakfast, Morgan proceeded with a selected number of the guests to one of the large conference rooms. The forum was Commander Nurmi's show, obviously well rehearsed and heavily loaded in his favor. Justin presented the same prospectus and reports on Argus Two that Morgan had heard once before, and the reaction was just as favorable. A few Jasprians expressed misgivings about safety, but Nurmi's team quickly reassured them.

There was no representative from Lumisland. Justin kept a stern eye on Morgan, and she made no waves.

Alia listened and took notes but said nothing. When the commander asked if she had questions, she shook her head. "Not yet. I have a lot to assimilate before I can even make an intelligent comment." She smiled. "It's been most interesting." She thanked the speakers and declared herself ready to see the city.

The envoy exuded energy, so crisp and fresh that Morgan could scarcely believe she was only hours off a hypership. But then, she was trained to diplomacy, Morgan told herself. Trained, too, she hoped, to listen fairly.

The afternoon hours dragged. Morgan lunched in her office and tried to catch up on more paperwork while she waited for her appointment, but she accomplished little. She couldn't concentrate on requisitions for new desks when what she had to say to Alia might influence the future of a planet.

Finally it was time. Commander Nurmi had given Alia the use of his office, and she received Morgan dwarfed behind the expanse of his desk. She motioned for Morgan to come around it, to a chair placed beside hers. "We can't talk with that . . . monolith between us," she said. "I suppose there's a function for such status symbols, but I've never been comfortable with them." She poured coffee and offered Morgan a cup. "This is *my* extravagance. Imported from Centauri Ceres. I carry it with me wherever I go."

Morgan accepted and sipped appreciatively. "The Jasprian version isn't very good," she admitted. "The soil, I think. The terraformers are still trying to improve it."

"A world built to order, eh? All safe and sane."

"Except for Lumisland."

"That's what I want to hear about. The snows. The people who live there." Alia clasped her hands and leaned toward Morgan. "The truth."

"I don't know if I can give you that," Morgan said. "I don't know it myself. I can only tell what happened to me, and if you want to know more, you'll have to make your own visit. You'll have to judge how important it is."

"Go ahead," Alia said.

Morgan's throat was dry when she finished. She hadn't intended to talk so long. Her allotted half hour had stretched to thrice that, with Alia waving away all interruptions.

The envoy had listened intently. "I thought there was something I wasn't being told," she said when Morgan stopped. "And I can understand why. Commander Nurmi has good reason to be nervous." She tapped her fingers on the desk top and fixed an inquiring gaze on Morgan. "What's your opinion? I won't ask if you think the psychic gifts are real; I can tell you do. But are they worth preserving? Balance them against the other benefits of Argus Two. The enormous new productive lands. Does one outweigh the other?"

Morgan shook her head firmly. "I'm not the one to tell you that. I can't. As I said before, you'll have to judge for yourself. Commander Nurmi thinks I can speak for Lumis-

land, but he'd be disappointed if I did. I can't say what he
wants to hear. The grubbers, as much as I saw of them,
seem to *like* living in the snow. But as far as Ahlwen and
his cult are concerned — most grubbers haven't any use for
them. They're afraid of him and his influence on their children.

"I'll say it again, though: I'm *not* an expert. I really think
you should go there and see the snow. Experience it. I think
you should talk to a lot of grubbers and visit one of Ahlwen's camps. Varma is out of bounds, but his camp near
First Station is easily accessible."

"Would they let me in?"

"Yes, I'm sure they would."

"Hmm." Alia resumed her finger tapping. "Could you
give me names of people up there who might be helpful?"
She stilled her hands abruptly, clasped them, and locked her
fingers. "Could you plan an itinerary for me? It can't be
longer than four days. I'll need guides, I suppose. I want to
stay in grubber camps, not the lodges. And I certainly want
to meet this man, Ahlwen. Can you arrange all this?"

It was what Morgan had hoped for, though she hadn't
expected Alia's decision to be so sudden. For a moment she
hesitated, until she thought of Vulpius. She could reach him
through Magnus, she was sure. "Yes, I can do it," she said.
"When can you go?"

"The sooner the better. I won't learn anything here, with
the short leash the commander has me on." Alia's jet black
button eyes twinkled. "You don't suppose he'll want to come
with me to Lumisland?"

The idea of the commander in a grubber camp made

Morgan smile, too. "Somehow I don't think so," she said.

"Then how about the day after tomorrow? I suppose I should make my hosts happy and trot around to a few more receptions first."

"I'll let you know," Morgan said. "I'll get on it right away."

They shook hands. Alia escorted Morgan to the outer office, where Commander Nurmi was trying to pacify two portly Jasprians wearing ceremonial robes and impatient frowns.

"Could I see you for a moment, Commander?" Alia asked. "I know I'm behind schedule, but this is important." She smiled at the Jasprians. "I'll be with you soon, gentlemen."

Morgan escaped to her own office, but not for long. In ten minutes Justin was there. "Lumisland! She wants to see the snow! What did you say to her, anyway?"

Morgan feigned innocence. "So she wants to do some sightseeing. Calm down. What's so alarming about that?"

Justin continued to steam. "That woman! Did you hear what happened on the city tour? We had purposely let the route leak out, and then changed it to mislead any demonstrators. But there was one small group in front of the mayor's house, and she had her driver stop. She actually invited one of them in to ride with her. One of those smelly independence freaks! He gave her an earful, too, according to the driver."

"She was bound to meet them. It's one of the reasons she came."

"Well, that goon couldn't have given her much of an impression. I'm not worried about him. But this Lumisland brainstorm. It'll upset all my scheduling! This week she was supposed to visit the central grainlands and the forest belt, the Grace Island fisheries and the Argus monitoring station. What am I supposed to do about it now? And what about the commander? He doesn't want to let her out of his sight, but . . . Lumisland?"

"That could be a problem," Morgan admitted. "Does she have to have an escort?"

"Of course! For security and . . . other reasons. If the commander doesn't go, I suppose it'll be me." He managed a tight smile. "At least I'd get to see Dee."

"You can try," Morgan said.

He started. "What does that mean?" The smile disappeared. "You hinted before at something concerning Dee. Let's have it."

"Sit down first."

He did.

Morgan took a deep breath. "Dee's joined a group in Lumisland. A sort of psychic sect. Followers of a man named Anders Ahlwen. Have you heard of him?"

Justin's face assured her that he had. "You can't be serious!" he exclaimed.

"I certainly am."

He paled, then flushed. "Yes, I've heard of the Ahlwenites. A bunch of kooks who claim the snow gives them superhuman powers. They've sent petitions against Argus Two, and they've even hired some influential Friislanders to speak up for them. They're well organized for a lunatic fringe.

"But Dee — how could you let her get mixed up in something like that? You knew her condition, how impressionable she was." His voice took on a hysterical note. "Or are you one of them? They got to you first, and you've sucked in Dee. Is that it? Have you been duping us all along, just to have a confidential chat with the envoy? You've sold out Earth, SEF, your own daughter —"

"Hey! That's enough! You're way out of line."

"Maybe. But you've got to admit, it sounds suspicious."

Morgan damped her own anger; there was no time for it. "Of course I'm not one of them. Don't you think I'd rather have Dee here, safe? We've tried, Arnie and I both, to get her away from Ahlwen's group. With no success at all."

"*I'll* do it." Justin's face was grim.

"You're certainly free to try. But you've got to act sensibly. Arnie went storming in like an avenging fury and nearly got himself killed. *Ask* to see her. You can get a message in to wherever she is. I'm pretty sure she'll agree."

Actually, Morgan wasn't so sure when she remembered Elsie's ineffectual efforts to see Britt. But perhaps Dee would react differently. She was so young. Perhaps she would want to see the handsome lieutenant again.

Justin continued to regard Morgan with suspicion. "It was poor judgment, taking Dee to Lumisland at all. If you recall, I was against it."

"Yes, you were," Morgan granted. "But I also remember just yesterday your saying that it was a good thing she was there and not here. None of us can predict the future."

"One thing I know for sure: I *am* going to Lumisland."

"Good. I was just about to start making the arrangements, at Alia's request. You can help. I suppose you can get a SEF plane?"

"For the envoy? No problem at all."

Justin left to arrange the transportation, and Morgan started on her own preparations. After several attempts to reach the Lumisatama Lodge, Morgan finally got through to Magnus. "Are you callin' for Arnie?" His voice was obscured by static.

"Yes, if he's there I'll talk to him," Morgan said, shouting. "But I really wanted to get a message to Vulpius."

The reception cleared. "Neither of 'em's here now," Magnus said. "They took a bunch of skiers to First Station. They'll be gone until tomorrow."

"I thought Arnie was driving the crawler."

"*Jo,* he's the relief driver. Days off, he goes out with Vulpius." Morgan could hear a chuckle. "Ball of fire, that one."

It was reassuring news, but Morgan had no time to dwell on it. She engaged rooms at the lodge for Alia and her party, for the first night. She explained to Magnus who Alia was, and what she wanted to see, and the lodgekeeper agreed that Vulpius could easily gain the envoy admittance to grubber camps. "They'll tell her, they don't want nothin' changed around here," he said. " 'Cept gettin' rid of that nut Ahlwen. What does she want to see him for, anyway?"

"You ask her that," Morgan said.

"I will. She's got no call to go chasin' after him. Everyone here knows what he is. 'Cept fools like Karla." He growled some more about swelled-headed crackpots who twisted kids' minds, until Morgan felt mired again in the sticky mud of Satama.

She hung up with relief. Vulpius would call her tomorrow, Magnus had promised. She hoped Arnie would talk to her, too, but she didn't dare expect too much. It sounded as if he were on an even keel again, but not as if he would be returning.

She supposed she should be happy for him.

She tried, but it didn't work. She crumpled up a paper and threw it across the room.

When she talked to Alia later in the day, to report on the arrangements, the envoy startled her with a new request. "I want you along, Morgan," she said. "I've talked to the commander, and there's no problem. It'll be you and me and Justin. Cozy, eh?"

18

"How many are in the sect?" Justin asked. He sat beside Morgan on the plane to Satama. Alia occupied the seat ahead.

Morgan hedged. "You mean actually living in the camps?" Justin had been plying her with questions that she didn't want to answer, particularly within Alia's range of hearing. The only way she could preserve a good conscience with both SEF and Ahlwen was to allow the envoy to draw her own unbiased conclusions.

"No, sympathizers, too," Justin said.

"I have no idea."

"But you can guess. You were there."

"I can't guess. I saw maybe thirty or forty people at Varma, but it's a warren of little rooms, and I never saw everyone together. The same with the First Station camp, and I don't know much about the Third Station one. I was only there briefly."

Justin persisted. "Would you say they're in the hundreds? Thousands?"

"I don't know! More like hundreds, probably. There aren't thousands in all of Lumisland."

"Do they have ceremonies? Argus-worship, that sort of thing?"

"I don't know, Justin." She must have said it a hundred times. "I don't think they have rites, or anything like that. Ahlwen is more a teacher than a religious leader. The people in his camps respect him, but he doesn't seem to exert power over them. I'm sure Dee could leave if she wanted to."

"If he has anyone underage, we can slap him with enticement of minors."

"I don't think he has."

"How about unlawful assembly? Does he have a license to preach?"

"In Lumisland? Who would care? Justin, you're barking up the wrong tree. Instead of going after Ahlwen, you'd do better to concentrate on Dee. You think she loves you. If it's true, that's all the ammunition you need."

Justin subsided, though he continued to dictate notes into his recorder. He pulled out a briefcase, and when his papers began to spread, moved to another seat.

Morgan wondered at the unlikely alliance she had formed with him. He wasn't remotely like anyone she would have chosen for Dee if she had the choice, but at least he deserved his chance. She didn't think he had much hope of success, but she wouldn't second-guess Dee. And she was through trying to shield her. Dee could deal with Justin.

Alia turned around in her seat. "You'll be happy to see your husband, won't you? Will he meet us?"

"Yes, he'll be driving the bus." Morgan assumed it, anyway. She didn't know what to expect from Arnie. They had talked briefly yesterday. At first Arnie had sounded affectionate and cheerful, his old self, but then she had told him about her impending visit. "Traveling in high company, aren't you?" he had said. After that, he had been coldly polite.

They descended, and Alia exclaimed over the first icebergs. Morgan had instructed the pilot to circle into the interior, but the snow colors were disappointingly muted by dark, low-lying clouds. They made a rough landing in the teeth of a sleet storm, dashed to the crawler under tarps, and collapsed, shivering.

The driver wasn't Arnie.

"We swapped days," the oilskin-caped grubber said when Morgan asked. "Magnus needed Arnie to take out some ski tourists."

"To First Station again?" Something hard and painful lodged in Morgan's chest. Arnie had certainly gone to lengths to avoid her.

"Naw, just around the mountain," the man answered. "First-timers. They'll be back for dinner." He squinted at Morgan. "You been here before, haven't you? You know Arnie down south?"

The lump grew heavier. He hadn't even spoken of her.

"She's his wife," Justin said in an exasperated tone. "And this lady who may come down with pneumonia is the special envoy from Earth. Can't you give us some heat in here?"

"I'm all right," Alia said. She pulled out sweaters from her carrybag. "Morgan, do you need one?"

"No, thank you." Morgan felt numb all over, but it suited

her mood. Nice welcome, Arnie, she thought. She brushed angrily at a wet trickle on her left cheek. She wouldn't let herself cry over him. At least not in public.

Their baggage came, and the bus pulled out. The driver gave a running travelogue, but they could see nothing through the sheeting gray rain. "Them skiers'll be back early," he said. "This storm'll be snow, other side of the mountain."

Alia peered through the window, trying to see. "Is it like this much of the time?" she asked.

The driver nodded. "*Jo,* that she is." He grinned. "Washes the mud every day, nice and clean."

"It's a perfect harbor," Justin said. "Better than Friishaven. Think of it, with an improved climate."

"Would you like that?" Alia asked the driver. "Warm, sunny days and grasslands beyond the mountains?"

He clamped his lips and frowned. "I dunno," he finally said. "I grew up in the snows. It's a lot different than this. Better. I wouldn't like to see it gone."

"Yet you're not living there now," Justin said. "Why not?"

The man shifted in his seat. He opened his window to spit. "Couldn't take the hard life," he said. He turned to glare at Justin. "But there's plenty who can. And me, I like to go back to my old camp every chance I get. Grasslands! Don't know nothin' about them!"

The crawler skidded on a turn, and the driver returned his attention to steering. Alia raised her eyebrows at Morgan and turned to Justin. "Your 'perfect harbor' probably wouldn't exist anymore," she reminded him. "Not according to the projections I saw. The new coastline would start with that mountain range."

Justin flushed. "Of course. I wasn't thinking.

"No great loss, though," he said, recovering quickly. "The harbor, I mean." They were in Satama, beginning the climb up the hill. "No one could possibly want to preserve this town."

The driver snorted. He opened his window again, and this time he left it down.

The rain blew in on the three passengers.

"That man. What an idiot!" Justin exclaimed when they were unloaded at the lodge. Magnus Borstrup commiserated with their damp condition and promised to bawl out the driver. He led them to the fire and brought them hot drinks in mugs. The lodge was warmer than Morgan remembered, almost comfortable.

"Everything is arranged," Magnus said. "Vulpius, he'll be here tomorrow, early. He's got three camps you can visit, all easy skiing."

"Ahlwen's, too?" Alia asked.

Magnus grimaced. "*Jo,* the one by Third Station. Ahlwen, he's up at the glacier now, but someone said he'd come down to see you. Though why you'd want to . . ." He glanced at Alia and shrugged.

"Did you send my message, too?" Justin asked. "The one to Dee Vernor?"

Magnus nodded. "I said I did it all. Everything."

Morgan hadn't expected it to be so easy. "Then you got an answer? From Dee herself?"

"No, not her," Magnus said. "I don't know who I talked to. It was a man. He said for you all to come, that it would take them two days to get down from the ice."

"I don't know what that means," Morgan said to Justin. "Dee may or may not be there."

"If she isn't, then she's not free," Justin said. "She'd want to see me."

Morgan sighed. She thought of Elsie, who had spoken almost the same words.

"You'll need a sled to get to Third Station," Magnus said. "I'll have it sent to Maakalascamp, where you'll be spending the night." He looked doubtfully at Alia. "You're sure that's what you want to do? It won't be what you're used to."

Alia smiled over the rim of her mug. "I know, and I *am* sure."

A jetsled whined to a stop outside, and Morgan heard a commotion on the porch. The outer door opened to admit Arnie and a noisy bunch of cold-bitten skiers.

They advanced on the fire. "What a storm. You won't get me out in that again!"

"My hands. I can't even feel them!"

"What's that you're drinking? Magnus, how about bringing us some."

Morgan moved aside. Arnie saw her, and a slow grin spread over his face. In seconds she was crushed in an embrace that lifted her from the floor. "I'm sorry I couldn't meet you," he said, and winked. "But I knew when I ordered up the storm that I wouldn't be out long."

One of the tourists overheard. "So you're responsible! Can you cancel the order? I'm here only for the weekend!"

"How long will it last?" asked another.

"It'll clear up in a couple of hours," Arnie said. "It always does. We'll go out again after dinner. You'll see — that's when the colors are best." He whispered to Morgan, "See what an expert I've become in less than a week?"

"You must go out tonight, too," Magnus said to Alia and Justin. "A bit of practice for tomorrow."

Morgan introduced Arnie to Alia. The lump in her chest was dissolving fast, but she cautioned herself to take it easy. Arnie could still disappoint her.

Alia finished her drink and refused another. "Justin and I are going out to visit the cannery," she said. "Magnus has offered to take us. I don't suppose you two would like to come along?"

Arnie and Morgan exchanged glances.

"No, thanks," Morgan said. "We'll see you at dinner."

The two settled in a corner, away from the boisterous tourists. "Have you heard from Dee?" Morgan asked at once.

"Not a word. But then, I didn't expect to."

Morgan admired Arnie's glow of good health. "I don't have to ask how *you* are. You look wonderful."

"The snows have been good to me. I had a lot of rebuilding to do, and I don't mean just my body."

"I was worried. You were so cold, when we talked on the phone."

"Not cold — scared. The idea of you hobnobbing with the envoy threw me, that you were in that class, and here I was, driving a bus."

"But you got over it." She searched his face. "You're coming back with me now, aren't you?"

"If you can stand my cooking again."

"Stand it! Let me tell you what Matt's been fixing." Morgan laughed, and the last of the numbing bitterness was gone.

The storm subsided, as Arnie had promised, in time for the late skiing.

Morgan joined the party. Behind the mountain, the final rays of Argus transformed the unbroken surface of the new snow to stained glass. When the first skiers shattered it, the fragments flew like a million sparks, then settled again into glowing ridges that bordered the vivid swaths of their passage.

Alia moved slowly, like a person entranced. "I can't believe it!" she exclaimed when Morgan came abreast of her. "I mean, I almost do believe — everything." She turned to face Argus and its sundog halos, standing motionless in silent wonder.

Magnus shouted, and Alia moved on. Morgan left her, to ski with Arnie.

He watched Justin, who raced ahead of Magnus with the easy coordination of a natural athlete. "Do you think he has any chance with Dee?" he asked.

Morgan studied the graceful figure, too. "I wouldn't care to predict," she said. "I think I know what *you'd* like, and I hope you won't feel too bad if it doesn't happen."

"I'd be disappointed, all right," Arnie admitted. "But I can handle it."

Morgan reached out a mittened hand and received a squeeze.

"Do you have to go off tomorrow?" Arnie asked. "What

230

would Alia say if you stayed here with me while she's visiting those camps?"

Morgan had been thinking along the same lines. "I don't think she'd care," she said. "She'll have Justin and Vulpius. I'm really not needed. But won't you be too busy to bother with a hanger-on?"

"You can come with me, if you don't mind riding around in the crawler."

"Okay," she said. "It's settled, then."

She looked back at Alia, who had paused again in homage to Argus. Yes, it *was* settled, she thought, relieved of a burden. Her role was finished. Whatever happened now to the snows and to Jaspre, it would be out of her hands.

Epilogue

The Farraday woman had done what he hoped, Anders thought as he observed the scene. She had brought him the one from Earth who would decide his fate.

His body reposed cross-legged on the floor of his meditation cell in Varma, but his inner sight ranged to its limits. Tiring from the effort, he left the skiers at Satama and returned to the surface of the glacier. A last inspection before he began his physical journey to the Third Station camp.

He found no danger to his flock. Argus shone undimmed to the southern edge of the ice, and north until it disappeared into eternal, frozen night. A storm threatened from the eastern sea ice, but it was a day's distance away. It would lose most of its force before it reached Varma, and as for his own travel, if he left at once he would encounter no problems.

He shortened his sight. Jacob and Ruben approached from the south, pulling a heavy sled over a bad patch of wave ice.

Anders flew to them, touched them with a welcome, and added his strength for a time to their efforts.

Closer to home, a dozen brothers and sisters opened their minds to Argus while they moved food between the two nearest caches. The young woman Dee, whose inner senses trembled on the brink of awakening, skied with them. An *elukka,* disturbed by their passage, bleated and raised a ravaged face to the sky.

He would speak to Dee again, Anders decided. She hadn't wanted to leave Varma to go to Third Station, but he knew that there would be no peace from the SEF lieutenant unless she agreed to a meeting. He sent a message to bring her in.

Ranging again, this time to the north, he looked in on his new adept where she crouched in her own cell under the ice. Her concentration was a glowing light around her, and he stayed without, unwilling to disturb it.

Britt had more than fulfilled her promise; her powers, he suspected, would rival his own. Anders wished he could be in Varma for her return, but the meeting with the Earth woman was too important.

He sought for a sign of what to expect. He had seen a veiled female figure many times before, in visions of his people's future, but she had not shown him her face.

He had to see this powerful woman from Earth, to know her, before the meeting. He withdrew from Britt's cell and rose again to the surface, to the mirror-smooth expanse of ice where Argus pooled its greatest strength.

Blinding colors glanced and shattered, then coalesced and formed patterns. They grew into images that spoke to him. Flames leaped over a creek bed where water clung in golden droplets to stones of green ice. A bird with six wings flew into the flames and out again, releasing a shower of burnt orange feathers that drifted over the snow. Where each one touched, a city sprang up, a magnificent Varma, populated by his new race, his children.

Beyond the fire, the veiled woman waited. Beside her appeared a second female figure, small, with bright black eyes, dressed in flowing draperies.

New flames rained from the sky, an inferno that threatened to engulf both Anders and his ice-walled cities.

Anders could not move. The black-eyed woman, whom he knew now for the Earth envoy, stood for a moment, uncertain. Then she unwound one of her draperies and cast it at the inferno, instantly smothering it. Glittering plumes of smoke arose, and when they dissipated, she was gone.

The veiled woman crossed the embers to join Anders. When she lifted her veil, he saw the face of Dee Vernor. A mature but still beautiful Dee. The pupils of her violet eyes reflected Argus in a glowing concentration of colors, and her expression was as serene as that of the most advanced adept. Around her danced small, ghostly figures with eyes like hers, and children's laughter tinkled in the icy air.

Anders closed his own eyes against the brightness. When he opened them, the ice walls of his room were solid around him. He touched each one, reassured that he and Varma were safe. So, he realized, was his new race, his vision of the future. Lumisland would indeed glow someday even without Argus, and until then, the snows would remain.